Little Grey Lies

THE FRENCH LIST

Little Grey Lies

HÉDI KADDOUR

TRANSLATED BY TERESA LAVENDER FAGAN

LONDON NEW YORK CALCUTTA

www.bibliofrance.in

This work has been published via the
Publication Assistance Programme Tagore,
with the support of Institut Français en
Inde/Ambassade de France en Inde.

The quotation from Ernst Toller's *Hinkemann* on pp. 54–5
is from *Brokenbrow: A Tragedy by Ernst Toller*
(Vera Mendel trans., with drawings by Georg Grosz)
(London: Nonesuch Press, 1926), p. 50.

Seagull Books, 2017

First published in French as *Savoir-Vivre*
© Editions Gallimard, Paris, 2010

English translation © Teresa Lavender Fagan, 2013

First published in English translation by Seagull Books, 2013

ISBN   978 0 8574 2 486 0

British Library Cataloguing-in-Publication Data
A catalogue record for this book is available from the British Library.

Typeset in Adobe Garamond by Seagull Books, Calcutta, India
Printed and bound by Maple Press, York, Pennsylvania, USA

PART I

The Parade

1

London, August 1930. Max was on assignment for *Excelsior*. He took advantage of the opportunity to meet Lena Hellström, his American friend, just in from Berlin. She was beautiful, wearing a blue and yellow dress. A shameless yellow, remarked Max. 'When is your piece coming out?' she asked.

'Not right away. In fact, I don't have a specific assignment, not really. I'm just looking for a rather juicy story, something with an English flavour, with a real twist at the end. I might do something else with it.'

They were wandering around London. Lena was in town rehearsing for a series of recitals and she was supposed to get some fresh air for two hours every day. Max liked walking with her but not for too long. She walked as if she were in the hills of her native Montana, and after a while Max's left ankle began to throb. Lena knew that. But she pointed out that if he couldn't keep up with her it was because she was taller. Mr Max Goffard was just a little man. Lena didn't add 'arrogant'. She looked at the Frenchman with affection, at his round face and his ears that stuck out, he made her laugh, she liked teasing him because he then became even funnier, she'd repeat 'little man' and Max would begin to think that people thought him arrogant and that made him angry. And Lena would talk about the anger of a little man. Her eyes would sparkle.

That afternoon, a long procession was winding its way through Whitehall, preventing them from crossing the road. Looking at the man who was walking at its head, Max immediately thought, 'What a presence!'

Later he learnt the man's name: Strether, Colonel William Strether, a hero of the Battle of Mons, August 1914, Belgium. The parade was to commemorate that battle, to place a wreath on the Cenotaph, the war memorial in Whitehall. To bring back a bit of the past for the dead who no longer had one.

The procession was coming from Trafalgar Square, wearing workers' caps, bowlers, officers' hats, festooned with decorations, one-armed men, cripples in small three-wheeled invalid carts, the blind holding on to the shoulders of the one-armed—all soldiers, their faces taut, their eyes staring straight ahead.

It was strange, these men had won a war and yet they had the clenched jaws of those sought revenge.

2

The procession through Whitehall certainly had style, with its neat rows of six men who stood straighter as they drew closer to the Cenotaph. They limped less, they tried to appear as irreproachable as their leader who was controlling them out of the corner of his eye. They followed his pace, their gait increasingly machine-like.

Suddenly, one of the invalid carts lost its front wheel. It was placed on the side of the road and repaired, while two men helped the one who'd lost his legs, he didn't want to sit on the ground, they picked him up under his arms and held him at their level, three men facing forward and an empty space under the man in the middle. Sometimes the legs of another man could be seen behind him, filling the void.

Strether was walking on the left of the first row, on the outside, the leader. Almost six feet tall, his chin sticking out, his eyes looking sideways, the leader. A single medal on his chest, a pewter-grey suit. No, Max had answered Lena, that's not the *Victoria Cross*, the *Victoria Cross* is usually pinned to coffins.

On the sidewalk across the road from Max and Lena, two onlookers—a short man and a fat one, wrinkled suits, bow ties and bowlers—stuck out their arms. The fat man's just above the shoulder of the short one. It was comical. It was in fact the Fascist salute. The crowd didn't say anything to them but no one else followed their lead. The English have a somewhat strict protocol for commemorations, and people respected it, even if this wasn't a true commemoration, even if in the minds of many it should have been held for something

3

else, to show the communists, for example, all the Reds, that there was a crowd in front of them, in the street, to defend King and Country and Empire.

The veterans paraded calmly, with unfailing order, to demonstrate what order in a society should be like. They paraded, their steps pounding like iron hammers, in a chic quarter, to show that all quarters can be beautiful, without laundry on the balconies, with only pure thoughts in everyone's minds. One need only desire it. But there is no reason to make unnecessary gestures with one's arms.

3

It was summer, London in summer, the sun pleasantly hot, the air cooled by a slight wind from the east that wound its way up the Thames. The procession of veterans in black and grey contrasted with the crowd in bright-coloured clothing pressing together on the edges of the sidewalks. Lena's blue and yellow dress was the height of fashion, a fashion that emphasized the hips and the bust, the spirit of the 1930s. It was made of printed muslin, with a layered skirt, very soft. 'You're wearing muslin?' Max had asked. 'In Paris,' she had replied, 'they call this a "little nothing". The fashion today is not to appear too rich.'

While he lagged behind, Max took the opportunity to contemplate his friend's movements. She exaggerated them a bit, then turned round, pretended not to have noticed anything, asked him if *Pillicock* was already tired. Max didn't like that nickname but she knew he wouldn't protest, it was from the time she had welcomed him into her bed.

When they were side by side Max sometimes glanced at Lena's profile. She sensed it, lifted her chin a bit without turning towards him. She wanted to avoid his remarks, which could hurt. The worst was when they were sweet, when he said to her, 'You have a very subtle chin' or 'It's clear you like to laugh.'

It seemed the procession would never end.

Max first saw the wreath rather far off, it was at the end of the procession. It wasn't the usual sort, one of those arrangements that is carried in one's arms. This one was huge, borne on the shoulders of a dozen men, like a reliquary, rolling along as if on the sea. And in the centre of the wreath was a large image.

Max wondered what it could be. A painting of the church of Mons? Its ruins? That battle of August '14 had caused twelve thousand deaths in two days. Then the image began to resemble a cloud, a cloud in the middle of a large crown, then three clouds, large storm clouds, one next to the other. Lena began to laugh. Could this be a tribute to the weather?

She had said that in French. Max didn't respond. A fat spectator on her left, with a pink, wrinkled face and sideburns, looked at her sideways, mutely saying, One doesn't laugh in front of a parade for King and Country! Max saw the man, sought and held his gaze. They heard the applause accompanying the passing of the wreath and the image. Joyless. The people were looking, they wanted to find out right away, a reliquary, a painting, the portrait of a hero? Or clouds? It was strange, those clouds on a painting under the August sun.

4

Lena looked at the man with the sideburns—he was shorter than she. Her doctor had explained that, on average, there is more than a ten-centimetre difference between the common people and those of the superior classes, a matter of nutrition and personal hygiene. She deliberately said a few words to Max in French. The man with the sideburns seemed to grow even angrier. Then she took Max's hand.

Lena took Max's hand right in the middle of White-hall and Max didn't know what that meant. It had been six months since Lena had taken his hand, he remembered, since she'd begun rehearsing with the pianist who seemed tenderly in love, her new accompanist. Max had never met anyone like him—a youthful build, barely twenty years old, looking like a pimp but with the mind of a vapid schoolgirl. His playing oozed sentimentality. Max had nicknamed him *Rubato*. The absolute opposite of Lena as far as music was concerned, but she had decided that he was to be her accompanist for the London recital. She claimed he had a great future and the hands of a Liszt. Max hadn't dared ask her whether they were just as appealing on the piano.

Maybe Lena was done with Rubato, and Max would have a chance to return to her bed. Or maybe she was just putting up a united front against this Englishman. Max had wanted to take Lena's hand since the beginning of the walk and she knew it, she walked in front of him as if it were a friendly stroll, old friends closing ranks before hostility, the way she took his hand implied things wouldn't go any further, I have someone else, Max, but we're still good friends, aren't we? Especially when a nasty Englishman is giving us the evil eye?

Then they were able to better see the clouds, vertical clouds, three grey masses. The spectators seemed ill at ease.

The battle of Mons, those were nights of bombings, the first real bombings for men who'd never known such a thing, until then they had only experienced the noise of great manoeuvres, shells that resembled those used in the Napoleonic wars. This was something else, eardrums shattered, the ground rose up, huge plumes of earth and smoke rose into the sky, clouds made by men, those must be the clouds in the painting. They must be, but they aren't. They are figures, figures that resemble human beings, three human-shaped clouds?

5

Strether stopped not far from Max and Lena, between them and the monument to the dead, he let the men march in front of him as they went on to form a double path of honour, three rows on either side of the road. Max watched him again, his demeanour a model of military bearing. 'A handsome man,' said Lena, smiling.

Pointing at the clouds in the centre of the wreath, Max said, 'They could be the three wise men.' Lena replied that, if so, that night in Mons they'd brought strange gifts. She said that in English, without smiling. Another look from the man with the sideburns, Max burst out laughing, Lena squeezed Max's hand again, people applauded. Those clouds really did look human, one sensed something military, clouds as soldiers, foot soldiers, the English infantry, unwavering. And the Englishman with sideburns looked at Max and Lena as if they were Napoleon's cavalry facing Wellington's troops at Waterloo.

It's funny, in these early years of the 1930s, a Frenchman and his American friend are watching a parade, they are smiling while they think about the clouds, a few years after the Great War, an Allied victory, and there's an Englishman next to them staring as if he'd like to strike them dead.

And Max wonders why, the guy even frowns with distaste while he looks at Lena, as if it were shameful for an American woman to be strolling with a Frenchman. Strange times . . . Recently, in the news, there was a story concerning customs, a headline war, the English customs officers in Dover and Southampton were subjecting French women to thorough controls, said the *Times*, to unjustifiable body searches, said *Le Matin*, in three columns on Page One. And the French editorials demanded *the same*. Several days of huge headlines and the end of the Entente Cordiale.

With a story of money behind all that. The English quickly want to reconcile with Germany, forget its war debts to better sell their merchandise over there. France doesn't agree. Germany will pay, say the French. And in fact, regarding payment, the Americans are beginning to demand that France pay back its debts to them. And the English are supporting that, discreetly. Everyone is talking about betrayal. That's why that guy's looking at me as if he wants to shoot me. And why you find customs officers' hands where they shouldn't be.

6

Lena has had enough of the Englishman with sideburns, enough of the parade. She'd gone out for a walk round the city, the parks, along the banks of the Thames, it was nice out, she wasn't going to waste her time watching a procession of gloomy, battered men. Should she pull Max by the sleeve? That's not done, silence would be more effective, create a silent void, sullen, no, not sullen, they hadn't gotten to that point, rather a dignified silence, a true woman's silence, with a bit of scorn, but Max would use that scorn to do his bit as the abandoned lover, sadness, or, better, a simple void, she's waiting, she's bored, no stupid sighing, no nervous fiddling with the parasol, she'll just create an empty space on the sidewalk, in Whitehall, one makes sacrifices.

But why should she sacrifice herself to the whims of a man? In order not to spoil this outing? It *is* being spoilt, with the sound of boots marching, old men, staying there, standing, stupidly waiting, a nice stroll, *I shouldn't have to sacrifice myself, sacrifice is an old person's idea, Max isn't moving, his eyes are fixed on the veterans, he isn't looking at me, I really wanted to take a walk and not see a parade, a walk in the park, with a lake, grass, pine cones, amusing encounters like the day before yesterday, the King's two little granddaughters on their tricycles, each with her governess, the boldest was the eldest, the one named Elizabeth, she went faster on purpose, to make her governess run, she was laughing, we could have taken a boat ride, it's hot, I can't stand the strap of my hat, I could just go to Hyde Park, fifty-fifty chance he'll follow me, pouting, or that I'll be alone, Thibault won't be there before tomorrow, I don't want to be alone and thinking of how my recital's become the opposite of what I wanted it to be.*

7

What if I just walk away, leave Max and his parade, it would be up to Max to follow, pouting, no he won't pout, he's not like that, if I leave he will follow, smiling, a tender, disarming smile, and we will stroll in Hyde Park, I will hold his arm, that will make him happy, and I will slow down, he will be nice, he will stumble a bit trying to keep up with me, he will suggest that we take a boat ride, or have some ice cream, or both, as one would offer them to a child, he will tell me his stories, he only likes racy stories, and he will watch for the opportunity to have his revenge, no, he won't do that, that would make him unhappy, Max is spontaneous, simply incapable of missing an opportunity to strike back, and life offers so many of those, he doesn't need to seek them out, there will be dinner, a restaurant, he will choose the restaurant, he will choose the dishes, or rather he will let me choose, he knows I always take a long time to choose, that's where it will happen, a lovely restaurant, no, Max, not inside, too much smoke, on the terrace outside, in the fresh air, it's nice out, Max will protest, he doesn't want to eat dinner with wasps and flies, he's in a bad mood, we'll end up sitting on the terrace.

8

At the restaurant we will be sitting across from one another, I will hesitate, Max will speak in a soft voice, he will have forgotten the incident at the parade, he will set down his menu, will wait, will say, 'Lena, we are wasting time,' in fact, he won't say that, he is French, but cautious, and if he said that I could reply, 'I've been wasting it for hours,' he won't say that, he will punish me, without seeming to, with a smile, 'There is a human being who is waiting for your order, my dear,' that would mean that I am disrespecting the waiters, a class prejudice, the patrician of the East Coast, but he knows that isn't true, and I will order something, anything, quickly, so as not to provide him with a pretext, and I will be unhappy with myself the entire evening, with food that will bloat me. He will smile, 'You don't like this fried food? Is it the mayonnaise? It tastes funny, doesn't it?' if he says the word mayonnaise one more time I will hurl my plate in his face, 'Do you want to order something else?' he knows that I would never do such a thing, he will give me no pretext to raise my voice, fried calamari, in the month of August, I will be angry at myself, women who don't like veterans parades have only one alternative—to endure them or to end the evening feeling bloated and ugly.

9

It was only when the wreath passed in front of them that the spectators saw the image clearly, not clouds, not a landscape, not human beings. Lena and Max couldn't understand. Round them the people grew sombre, they were wearing festive colours but were becoming sombre, even the woman to the left of Max, wearing colours as bright as a cockatoo, her eyes brimming with tears.

The wreath arrived in front of Max and Lena. The Englishman with sideburns removed his hat, saluted, then turned towards the couple and said in French, 'Ce sont les anges!'

Max hadn't asked him anything, the man hadn't said 'angels' but '*the* angels.' He looked Max in the eyes while he spoke French. It wasn't the moment to laugh, to assume the air of a sarcastic Frenchie who isn't surprised by anything the English do, we hadn't asked him anything, he didn't say *angels* but *the* angels, three angels in the middle of the painting, the man with sideburns stared at Max while he spoke French, Max looked at the angels, three tall figures, not chubby angels, not angels with little breasts like those on the ceilings of Versailles, no, no ambiguous gender, real men.

10

They were warrior angels, three angels standing in the middle of the painting, in the middle of a battlefield, opposite the Prussians, three exterminating angels as tall as Strether, standing as if on real legs, a broken cannon at their feet, a destroyed church behind them, large dark clouds that became grey angels, without light, hollow eyes, with shadows under their eyes, the colour of the end of the world, holding bows as tall as they upright beside them, three angels seen at three-quarters view, large wings folded on their backs, who forced the German soldiers to turn round and flee, some with their arms raised in the air.

And behind the angels are English soldiers falling back in an orderly fashion, in a column, their weapons on their shoulders, as if returning from a review.

The man with sideburns continued to stare at Max while pointing at the angels. On the cobblestones heels clicked even more mechanically, the man said softly, under his breath, 'That day they came from Azincourt!' Max understood that he was thinking—and too bad for your cavalry smitten by our bowmen. 'Azincourt was five centuries ago, wasn't it?' the man added. He pointed at Strether who was standing still, who was saluting the angels as though he were the colonel of the best infantry in the world. 'That man knows everything!' he said.

Strether was standing erect with tears in his eyes.

11

While she was in London, Lena worked every day with Thibault, her young accompanist and lover. Some friends of Lena had left her their house for the duration of her stay, a beautiful house in the Bloomsbury quarter, a drawing room on the first floor with a glass rotunda, bookshelves of blond wood spanning some fifteen metres, a beautiful baby grand in perfect condition and a western view onto an interior garden.

They clashed immediately over the first lied, over a question of tempo, tempo often a point of contention.

'It's the song of their first encounter, Thibault, it's a woman who is singing her love at first sight.'

Thibault was playing almost *largo*, pouring out his heart—*Seit ich ihn gesehen*, since I saw him. Lena didn't like that *largo*.

'Look at the score, *larghetto*, Schumann writes, it's faster, there's surprise, it's not a complacent meditation.'

Thibault didn't react to 'complacent' and made a point of playing faster than *larghetto*, almost *andante*.

'No, Thibault, that's too fast, you know it, there are dreamy, obscure qualities, you have to let them rise to the surface.'

Lena was looking at Thibault, his long hair, the sharp profile, *fifteen years between us, he's toying with that, sometimes he plays the naughty boy, sometimes the offended man, the love and life of a woman*, Seh ich ihn allein, *I see only him, what is that called, that irony when I look at him, that pain when he tells me he will be away tomorrow, I'm not the type to ask for explanations, I would like to be able to lock Thibault in this apartment and go out when I want, come back to see him when I want, this lied is a springtime love but I'm in the month of August.*

Lena was thirty-five, but since she'd been with Thibault she felt much older.

'*Larghetto*, Thibault, let's listen to the score, only the score, yes, I am a purist, *I mustn't tell him what I feel when I see him walking across the garden, if Max saw me watching him from a window I wouldn't hear the end of it*, no, make the chords stand out more, not imitation, it's Schumann, Thibault, a blindness that moves to dreaming, there's no reason to get angry, I'm not scolding you, you are as good a musician as I am, we will work it out together, ok, let's try it your way, forget what I said.'

Knowing she was fighting a losing battle, Lena gave in to her lover's whims and calmed herself by watching the sunlight bathing the books on the bookshelves.

12

None of their rehearsals occurred without friction. The first lied of *Frauenliebe und Leben* had become sentimental. Claude, Thibault's agent, had come by to listen, he said he was thrilled, the audience was going to love it, the spring of love, all the women would rediscover their youth in it, he had said that looking at Lena and Lena hadn't reacted. She had again wanted to say what she read in the poem and the notes, 'A circular structure, Thibault, this budding love opens and closes with *I think I am blind*, there are two things, two registers, what she imagines, her impulses, and what the poem and the music tell us behind what she believes, that's the tension of the lied, she believes something, and certain words, certain notes say there will be something else.'

Thibault had thrown his arms up in the air, looked at his agent conspiratorially, 'Do you think the audience can hear circular structures and different registers? They listen to the feeling, to the emotion, our duty is to give them feeling, not circular structures, it's our duty, Lena!'

Lena didn't respond, kept her thoughts to herself, *that little bastard has the gall to talk to me of duty, from the depths of his complacency.*

'No, Thibault, wait a minute, don't shout, I was just making a suggestion, no, I didn't mean complacent, I said it was pleasant, let's start again' *wait, for now I love him, they call that love, I have to wait.*

Lena began to sing again, followed the piano, its complacency, relaxed in spite of herself, somewhat ashamed. Thibault said, 'So there we are,' stood up, kissed Lena's hand, she pretended to try to pull it away, *why does his kissing my hand affect me that way? The agent must think he's done here, it's almost five o'clock.*

'I'm sorry, I was about to . . . What were you saying, Thibault?'

'Yes, we're going out now, Lena, Claude and I have a meeting, a possible recital, in Leeds, a solo, that's the advantage pianists have, we can play alone.'

His satisfaction made Thibault look the way he would in thirty years.

'But that's wonderful, Thibault, bravo! I'm really happy for you!' *He's going to play alone, don't tell him it is probably by chance, two days after our posters were put up, that he was called for recitals, at twenty years old, and he plays as if he were seventeen.* 'But Leeds is wonderful, Thibault, you should have told me.'

And Lena didn't tell Thibault that Leeds was horrible.

13

A cerebral love, that's what Thibault said to Lena when he wanted to cause trouble, she was experiencing only a cerebral love, she was incapable of truly loving anyone or of finding the right tone for it.

She wanted to prove him wrong, the second lied, at least a pure song, she just had to let herself go, *Er, der Herrlichste von allen*, he, the most magnificent of all, Lena thought that Thibault was *herrlich* too, *his lips, his eyelashes, his neck, why do I love his neck so much? He seems happy, it is easy to follow him here, these rhymes are easy*, gut, *what is good*, Mut, *courage, I just have to follow, a simple momentum, and each time I'm silent the piano takes me off again, it's sweet, cadence, modulation, joyful tears, more rhymes*, Schein, *the luminous appearance, reconciled with* sein, *somewhat easy the being and the appearance, but sometimes it is good to take, and he loves me, why isn't he looking at me? We could be as one, looking into each other's eyes*, niedre Magd, *the humble servant, it's a bit much, but isn't that how I feel when I ask him if he's hungry, if he's thirsty, when I enjoy dressing him?*

14

'No, Thibault, we have to do that again, "only to be overcome and sad," the third stanza, the end of the stanza!' *What is wrong with me? I should be quiet, no, the music wants to speak, and he is a wandering minstrel.* 'Schumann wrote *ritardando*, Thibault, don't look at me like that, just there, *Selig nur und traurig sein*, I need nuance, *sein*, a dotted half-note, it's the only place where you don't have a piano transition, I simply mean that for a fraction of a second we're not in simple emotion, being overcome and sad, there's a tension, it is contradictory, no, I'm not splitting hairs.' *There you go, he's mad, keep a happy voice, relaxed, don't be dramatic, we are two artists at work, conflicts resolve themselves.* 'Happiness and sadness together, Thibault, it's really an unstable mixture, ok, we'll do it your way, but I think we could convey that the emotion is not that simple, it's not coldness, don't you ever feel that mixture of the two at the same time? *Selig, traurig,* you're being mean, you didn't have to answer "Yes, Mother," fine, let's move on, as you wish, emotion, no, I didn't murmur' *boy oh boy* 'ok, I might have thought it but it was to get back at you, in fact I wasn't thinking that, no, I don't think you're an idiot, we'll do it your way, no, you're wrong but we'll do it your way, yes, you're right, yes, I do like to kiss your neck, does it bother you?' *He doesn't like that, my somewhat greedy gestures, he wants to be the only one to have them, he needs only to have them more often.*

15

'Let's start over, Thibault, the fourth lied, the ring on the finger, *Du Ring an meinem Finger*, you're right, it's a circle, you're the one who said it this time, it's even obvious, no, I'm not saying that you only say obvious things, I do the same, come on, let's start over, I assure you I wasn't implying anything, the final stanza repeats the first, an overlapping of stanzas, overlap me, what time is it? The ring that opens the lover's eyes, that really brings her out of her dream, that's why women like rings, Thibault, because they bring us out of a dream for an even sweeter reality, will you give me a ring?'

And Lena was immediately angry at herself for having asked such a thing, even as a joke, *don't tell him that if he wants I'll lend him the money, he's not answering, I should insist on the ring, otherwise he'll think I'm thinking of the money that I loan him, he's acting as if he didn't hear, I shouldn't have asked for a ring, I'm exasperating him, I can't stop exasperating him, yet I didn't say anything, yes, I mentioned a ring but I didn't say enough. I should have insisted on the ring, played the silly girl, now he knows what I think, I don't want to think such things,* 'You, with the ring on my finger, you have opened my eyes,' *he's overdoing it, he's using too much pedal.*

'A little softer on the piano, perhaps, the right hand, Thibault, it is simply repeating the song from start to finish' *it's good I didn't say* 'not so loud.'

21

16

'Yes, I do want to be more expressive, yes, our young woman is experiencing pleasure, loving piety, do you believe in loving piety? She is his servant, you think she's stupid? Men don't like women who want to serve? We love that, you know, *Ihm angehören ganz*, all together, *ganz* belong to him entirely' *that's a lie, I hate belonging, especially to a dance-hall pianist, but I love him, I can't help it, I need a little time* 'and you hear? Another rhyme, *ganz* and *Glanz*, the splendour of the lover, it's kitsch? You're right, we should play it kitsch. It's complicated' *here we go, I'm getting into complicated again, instead of being quiet, but I can't let it go,* 'it seems to be kitsch, Thibault, but in the background there's a ruse of devotion, I'm not trying to be an intellectual, it's a ruse, it's German romanticism, a woman who gives herself entirely, such a gift creates an obligation, the one who receives it should be deserving of such a gift, he should prove to be dazzling, it's a bit heavy to bear, the splendour, *Glanz*.'

Thibault didn't respond, he was pouting. Lena regretted talking so much, *the compensation for the gift, they're going to tell me again that such reflections aren't womanly, I should smile, kiss him, ask him to put his hands on me, a ruse of devotion, that's great!*

17

It was around five in the afternoon when they finished working, the time when they could be together, but more and more often Thibault had something to do, he went out, like a thief, as quickly as he could.

Lena had learnt to read the signs, the way he had of moving closer to the door while talking to her sweetly, the first few times she'd been taken by surprise, then she'd adapted, tried to control the situation by moving closer to the space in front of the door. Thibault had to get by her to leave.

She didn't appear to be preventing his exit, she smiled, complimented Thibault, she knew he wouldn't dare say 'I have to go' before being able to do so right after saying those sweet words, it was a challenge, a territory of a few square metres in front of the door, she quickly went to stake her place while talking to him gently, he acted as if he was going to stay for hours in the apartment, he moved away, answered, even went to the window, on the other side of the room, she didn't fall into the trap, didn't follow him, eventually put a large vase in the entrance with gladioli and birds of paradise, tending to them gave her a pretext, Thibault asked for something to drink.

'Oh, make yourself at home, you know where everything is, you have as much right as I do to use this house, I still don't understand why you live in the hotel' *if Max could see me . . .*

But there was always the moment when Thibault, his pupils black and his teeth white, decided to come towards her and kiss her, take her by the shoulders, hug her. Then turn her round so that she was in his arms but he was then the one closest to the door.

18

When Thibault had carried out the manoeuvre and his back was at the front door, he hugged Lena, then moved away, put his hands on her shoulders, her hips, caressed her, he was free to leave, he could linger.

She hated that, sometimes as soon as she saw him moving towards her she moved away, freed the passage, and he abandoned the charade. She stifled a 'You're leaving already?' and said instead 'You're leaving? Great, I have some errands to run.'

She left along with him, then was alone in the street, with the smells of gasoline, dog droppings, coal, did some shopping to avoid going home, was reluctant to call Max, Max's smile when he saw her arriving, she took his arm, he didn't say a thing.

She also sometimes stayed at home, ostensibly with a headache. *I'm not suffering, I'm not despairing at seeing Thibault go out, if he stayed I would get bored quickly, I often get bored with him, his conversation is high-school level, a high-school student who doesn't read, but I feel sick when I think that he might not return, another month of rehearsals, that's too long, it's stupid to mix pleasure and work, a week would have been enough, and Thibault is taking advantage of the time to go to Leeds, another month of half-hearted rehearsals, then six days of recitals, we've planned nothing afterwards, no other project, no tour, I don't want to think about it, no one has spoken of another project, he thinks he is on his way, that he no longer needs to be on stage with me, solo, the poor guy, in Leeds, he has no idea.*

Sometimes Thibault sensed that Lena was ready to leave him, sometimes he stayed and took her.

19

Once Lena had the feeling that Thibault was listening to what she was singing, staying behind her song, the third lied, *Ich kann's nicht fassen*. 'How could he have, among all others, chosen me, I who am so humble, and fulfil me?' the lied of the blessed death, *den seligsten Tod*.

'Perhaps a bit less obviously sensual on the keys, Thibault, since the words say it all, and then they are only series of eighth notes, right? No, I didn't say anything, you have a perfect right to your sensuality, even on the series of eighth notes.'

Thibault had asked to go back to this lied and had begun to listen to Lena, to let her speak as he had never done before.

'Oh, it is too beautiful to be loved, Thibault, she has been overwhelmed, *beglückt*, she can't believe it, she wants to have been dreaming, *Es hat ein Traum mich berückt*, a dream has bewitched me, *berückt, beglückt*, the secondary dominant for *berückt*, and the tonic, the effect of détente for *beglückt*, we are all like that, you men dream that this will happen, and you do everything to make it happen, and women, when it happens, dream that it's false, and do everything so it becomes so.' *What has come over me to say such things, generalities for a women's magazine! And he's listening to me, he is concentrating, it's sweet.* 'She's dreaming, Thibault, instead of simply enjoying reality.'

Lena paused, for the pleasure of hearing Thibault say to her, 'She's an idiot!'

'Maybe not as much an idiot as all that.'

More pleasure at seeing Thibault's face appear to be pondering the question, *it's a change from dissimulation.* She continued, '*O lass im Traume mich sterben*, oh, let me die while dreaming. The dream will allow her to dream of her death. If her lover's vow is only a dream, she might as well die, right?'

At the piano Thibault was no longer playing his feelings, he was trying to stay as close to the score as possible, he was almost playing it exactly.

Lena was so happy to see him being attentive that she did not immediately try to understand the reasons for such a change.

20

Lena no longer remembers when she finally understood why Thibault had become so attentive, it was perhaps when they arrived at *sterben*, when they went over *den seligsten Tod*, blessed death, but she isn't sure, it didn't happen on one word.

On 'blessed death' there was only a sign, the revelation came later, when an image came to her, an image and a cry, then she understood everything, she was able to reconstruct everything. A hateful image.

There had been small warning signs, at the time not given the importance they deserved, at first a silence. *I should have paid more attention to that, a drawing-room conversation, Thibault's silence in a drawing room, he who usually loves to dominate conversations wherever he is, here he was silent.*

And Lena sees herself with Thibault round a tea service and a plate of scones, they'd been invited by that novelist, a woman of formidable intelligence, who looked like a goat but with formidable intelligence, that was her reputation, and a horrendous gossip, Thibault listened to that woman intently, and it amused Lena, one sensed that he wanted to say something but didn't dare, he was afraid of saying something stupid.

And Lena said to herself that she should have been more attentive instead of being amused at the spectacle of Thibault and the novelist *and now I'm no longer amused, he is listening to me like someone who is recording a lesson that he will use somewhere else, instead of his own stupidities he is going to use my words with that novelist with the long face and skinny arms, with the huge blue eyes.*

'Yes,' Lena had said then in the car of the Maynes who were driving them home, 'huge blue eyes, when they closed the woman's face drooped.'

The Maynes had laughed a lot, but not Thibault. Lena had thought that in her lover's silence she had detected some cowardice.

21

Lena is speaking again of the third lied, she is already hearing her words repeated out of Thibault's mouth, in her absence, *he is over there, in that house in Hampstead, he is acting intelligent for that novelist who believes only in intelligence, he is using my words,* Lena continues to deliver him words he is incapable of producing, she knows she shouldn't do such a thing, *I am giving him what he needs to mount that goat, unless he already has.*

'This occurs round death, Thibault, *den seligsten Tod,* blessed death, loving death. And because she is dying, she has the right to say everything, everything a woman shouldn't say, she is dreaming of everything that women are forbidden to say and to feel, look at the last two words, *unendlicher Lust,* endless pleasure. In fact, what she wants is to die of pleasure.'

Lena looks for the idea of pleasure in her lover's eyes, she knows he will in turn look for it in the eyes of another while saying the same thing but she lets her humiliated and chatty love speak, 'It's the ruse of love, Thibault, the dream of death enables the dreamer to speak in complete freedom, she's going to die, so she has the right to savour her death, the young woman certainly deserves that much, to savour, *schlürfen*, it is almost an onomatopoeia, swallow one's death, those Germans have such precision, *schlürfen*, to drink noisily.'

Thibault has a lascivious look in his eye that Lena doesn't like, she interrupts, 'I forbid you from thinking such things, *schlürfen*, *in Tränen unendlicher Lust*, to drink in tears of infinite pleasure, that is why she is dreaming her death, to do what one doesn't speak of when one is a young woman, to die of infinite pleasure, it's good, isn't it? And it is the only way not to be considered a hysteric.'

And when she said 'infinite pleasure' the image she so hated flashed before her for the first time, and the cry, and the novelist who was drinking Thibault with her eyes. More than an image, a scene.

Thibault was listening, with an attention that was wrenching Lena's heart.

PART III

An Officer in Distress

22

It was by chance that Max saw Strether again, the man at the head of the parade in Whitehall, the one wearing a medal, a DSO, Distinguished Service Order, the one with tears in his eyes as the painting of the three angels passed by. It happened a few days after the parade, in the dining room of the Regent Hotel, where Max was dining with two French deputies who were passing through town, it was Strether who handed them their menus, he was the maître d', with the bearing of a prince, existing above the throngs, his head slightly bent but dignified, thin lips, a soft voice, he didn't take their order but dictated it to a server standing behind him, commented on the menu, assembled the meal while making the client feel he was doing it himself, signalled to the sommelier, wished them bon appétit, went back to his observation post. With his hands behind his back, accessible and dominating, he fit right into the vast dining room of the Regent, the one you arrived at by going down some dozen steps.

Those steps had the ability to put everyone in a good mood, the guests because they could see who was arriving and those who were arriving because they were descending from above.

The clientele was a somewhat mixed group of people, many dinner jackets but also some saris, turbans, the inevitable kilts, dresses, the savage infighting of dresses. There were a lot of Americans, dressed even more formally than the lords, speaking a bit too loudly.

The entire Empire was there, along with its many conflicts.

'Are you really going to release that anarchist Gandhi from prison?' a maharajah asked an administrator from the Colonial Office.

'The *Warspite*'s been sent off the coast of Calcutta.'

'Yes, the newspapers published photos of its guns, their shells weigh eight hundred kilos, those things can fire at whole neighbourhoods.'

'The American press is protesting, the entire world is watching us.'

'Oh, there'll be more regrettable events but we can't allow ourselves to be ruled by the natives. Do you think the French would allow that in Indochina and Africa?'

23

From time to time, in the huge dining room of the Regent, Strether lingered at certain tables, even those where there were foreigners, everything had its importance, and how did those foreigners manage to have such beautiful women at their tables? Not fools, either, real adult women, with ideas, money, notoriety and cigarette-holders—heiresses, an aviator, a skinny novelist, a doctor, a magazine owner. Strether answered questions, lingered for a moment at a table, full of deference for the men, blushing with the women, then, asking permission to wish his guests bon appétit, he stepped back smoothly, pivoted on one foot, moved the other in line by raising it off the ground, the toe pointing forward, and walked away as if he were following an order from the table he was leaving but with a movement whose very perfection rendered it supremely free.

It amused Max, watching the women who watched Strether moving among the tables—they pretended to look at their cigarettes or at the state of their lacquered nails but their glances went farther, rested on the neck and the shoulders of the maître d', the body of the soldier that was beginning to fill out, and they always ended in the same place, they thought they weren't being watched, it wouldn't have pleased Strether, one day I'll have to tell him, the glances always ended on his behind.

24

Leaving the restaurant, Max thanked the maître d', no, not thanked, that would have been condescending, he simply complimented him on the remarkable order that had reigned over the entire dinner, better, the harmony, and asked him straight out, with very French aplomb, if he would agree to talk about the battle of Mons, 'I really like those angels, they'd make a great story, a tribute to your battles, I promise I'll take no liberties.'

After his shift Strether joined Max for what would become a long series of evenings spent together drinking and talking, most often in the cocktail lounge of the hotel, with its wood panelling, draperies, deep arm-chairs, muted sounds. Max had his cognac, Strether ordered a beer and a whisky, sipped them one after the other.

When he spoke it was with the hoarse voice of someone who had shouted on the battlefields to gather his men, to try to bring the fallen back to life. He spoke of war and of the financial crisis, without Max under-standing where he actually stood on the issues, and he spoke about Mons, no, you couldn't really say he spoke about it, not in the sense of a beginning, an unfolding, a peak, a denouement, an end—no, Mons came to him haphazardly, night after night, between two cold smiles.

At first he didn't speak of the angels, and when Max brought them up he said, 'That's what they say,' with the look of someone who doesn't believe it but who, in his personal experience, must think it not entirely false. If he doesn't say anything, it's because a Frenchman needs a little initiation period, it's not disrespect, it's caution.

He spoke about Mons, 11.30 p.m., the trembling of the men when they understood that the Germans were going to attack again, in large waves, in the dark of night, with groups of advanced troops, exposed one by one to the entire enemy army, the officers recovered what they could, sent men back out breathlessly, whereas half the corps had already disbanded, part of the other half returning running, each man for himself, opening fire pell-mell, impossible to recognize anyone, to fill in the gaps, a battle where only the deserters could win.

In the bar, past 1.30 a.m., Max latched onto snippets of Strether's story so he wouldn't think of Lena and her pianist.

25

Night, at Mons. To the left of the front, a panicked liaison officer brings an order to retreat to the Welsh, he says everything to the Prussians thinking they are the Welsh, the Prussians send him to a prisoner of war camp in Pomerania where he later hangs himself.

Things calm down a bit, the men try to eat, death upsets the mess kits, mouths are filled with dirt, the brown odour of death brought on the breath of the wind, the sound of rustling grass, it is night, bodies brutally spread out by the hail of bullets, they stumble, fall into a hole, a soldier emerges from the next hole, joins you, you're crazy, the machine guns, you should have stayed, no, couldn't, I was with Stephen, only a part of Stephen, you don't think of anything any more, someone calls, the rest of the group has disappeared, the earth is crawling with crying, the anger of cannons, you don't know where you are any more, a brilliant explosion lights up the bodies caught in barbed wire, they are called the darlings of glory.

Here Strether paused, looked at the bar, the room, then at Lena who, after the second evening, had joined them, he hesitated. To describe his war to this woman? Lena seemed neutral, Max could see from Strether's looks that he found her very beautiful and, gradually, Strether resumed, you understand it's Hell, someone asks where Christ went, a mocking voice says that he's in no-man's-land, other voices swear in the mire, you come out of holes, you find the group, you divide up into other holes, like animals, huddling, a wounded man whose head soaks his neighbour's shoulder with blood, there aren't trenches yet, in the morning you'll also see poppies.

Strether looked at Lena, the beautiful expanse of skin, the same tone from the forehead to the plunging neckline, cheeks, shoulders, throat, a seamless background for the dark red spot of her lips, 'Your colonel really knows women,' she'll tell Max later, 'when he looks he really lingers, he sees everything, even the make-up.'

A man suddenly sees a little bend in the road, a thatch roof, they need to wash off the wheels of the cart, a blue vase, primroses, curtains, a soft voice, the soup smells good, he is awakened by the shaking of a comrade, convulsions in the mud, licking dried lips, trembling, the comrade's mouth covered in blood, I'm dreaming, the curtains, I'm going to wake up at home, the night filled with terror and the sleeper returns to his sleep of death.

Lena found Strether interesting. His hands were more delicate than one would expect for a warrior.

26

The battle of Mons, August 1914, we are nothing but a block of hatred and fear in the night, a voice stands out, do you think we're here by mistake? Orders fly, bayonets, someone vomits, no one knows how rotten he is before giving in, careful, *in three minutes* an officer says, then *forward*, you run, two men hang back, run on when a sergeant threatens them with his revolver, they lunge, wanting to kill the sergeant, later it will be called *patriotic consent*, the back of a comrade torn to shreds as if by a monstrous claw, and while writing that, rereading it, Max decides to edit *as if by a claw*, it's grammatical padding, he must get rid of *as if*, write *a back torn to shreds by a monstrous claw*, or a dry description, *sprayed with blood, the spine exposed, skin, open-air dissection, it's trembling, increasingly massive explosions,* and he will want to replace *torn to shreds* with *stripped,* which isn't as strong, but, indeed, *torn to shreds,* that says too much, it already implies a claw.

'Your tone is pretty good,' Mérien, his editor in chief, will tell him, 'how did you come up with it— from Strether, from other accounts, from novels?'

'Everywhere, and I've tried to condense, to capture, to create, to gather, to cut, but without doing too much staging. At Mons there was panic that night, not everywhere, but some units, soldiers deserted quicker and quicker, a man was propelled by a mortar shell, thrown through the air, his arse exposed, a Scotsman in a kilt.'

'No, Max, spare us the arse and the kilt.'

'I swear it's true, it's a real soldier's story, I did a real investigation, a real letter from a soldier, it happened just like that, a Scotsman who wasn't wearing anything under his kilt.'

'Take out the Scotsman, true or not, get rid of him.'

'You're old-fashioned, boss, you don't want people to see a man's arse in the midst of a battle, is it the pale white that bothers you, the softness?'

'That's not the issue, it's simply too much, it's too predictable, the eternal story of the Scotsman naked under his kilt, it might be true but it sounds like a circus stunt, the reader will know what's coming, very bad, it breaks the sense of reality. If you really want an arse, put in the glance of an American woman who lingers over the posterior of your maître d'—you've already done it? Then don't ruin your battle with the Scotsman's arse, go on, the parade, Whitehall, the battle, quickly or maybe Lena's lover, love is more consensual than your crazy battles.'

27

At the Regent, during their conversations, Strether didn't drink as much as Max. Max ended up having a bottle of cognac, quickly advancing to his third glass and beyond, Strenther drank only the two glasses he'd ordered, alternating between beer and whisky, often bringing the glass to his lips but not really swallowing, a man with a lot of self-control.

At Mons, orders had forced the troops to counter-attack, the counter-attacks were quickly swallowed up by the German mass, soldiers ran in the opposite direction, they had to give a general order to retreat to avoid a stampede, Wellington's army turned tail for the first time in a century, in a great strategic battle, not a small unit somewhere in Africa, no, an entire army corps turning tail, you can see why I wanted to include my Scotsman and his kilt in Strether's story, it's funny, when English historians tell the story, they turn it into a victory, and it's commemorated with angels, why?

Strether's pale blue gaze went from one bar fixture to another, greeted a few patrons, returned to Max, to

Lena. At the beginning, he said, there was a story of angels riding white horses, a tale, it was a rumour that spread through the Second Corps, you have to understand that Mons was a retreat, a defeat, the image that would weigh on everyone was that of English soldiers retreating from the enemy over close to one hundred miles, leaving behind thousands of wounded, it's not very good, whereas an angel, several angels on horseback, charging the enemy to relieve our troops, that would be acceptable, the Germans were the devil, everyone agreed on that, it was normal that the English would be aided by the angels, but the horses . . . Strether frowned with distaste, the scorn of an officer in the infantry for the cavalry.

28

In the bar of the Regent, Strether caught Lena's gaze more and more frequently, Lena smiled, he got carried away with his story of the battle and of the angels, sometimes interrupting himself as if he didn't believe it himself, as if to give some space to another Strether whose strong mind would have objected to that legend. Have you ever seen angels on horseback? For what? Divine horses? It was a fable for weak people, horses, cavalry, it wasn't done to force a decision, don't forget that they were also talking about infantry angels.

At the angels' feet were many English cadavers, though, you have to understand what happened, at first they didn't talk about angels, at first they spoke of archers who would have intervened, confronted the Germans, to cover our retreat, archers who came directly from Azincourt to Mons.

At that Lena interrupted Strether and told him the story of the Englishman with sideburns, who had, in a rather aggressive tone, mentioned Azincourt to Max.

Yes, said Strether, they talk a lot about those archers of five centuries ago, but archers are pagan creatures, and our Great War was very pious, from the beginning, so they turned the archers into angels, the angels belonging to God, if they helped the English it means the English retreated through God's will, it is no longer a defeat, the angels with bows of archers make everyone happy, Azincourt and divine Will, but it's an invention, there were no angels, it was an alliance between people who wanted to have seen them and people who wanted to believe.

Lena liked Strether's idea, she told him so.

On their walk the next day Max teased Lena a bit about that exchange with Strether, 'The colonel smiled when you complimented his idea, it's amusing, those soldiers who acknowledge the intelligence of women when it underscores their own.'

Lena didn't say anything and Max didn't pursue it.

29

Strether spent some time on the subjects of angels and credulity, he saw Max and Lena almost every night.

Max finally got to work on his story, and Strether, without saying anything, behaved like a man who has understood that someone wants to paint his portrait at the same time as tell the story of the battle of Mons, he didn't say anything about it and from time to time gave a mixture of information and enigma that renewed Max's desire to describe the man.

They left the Regent a bit past one in the morning. The three of them walked to sober up, walking up to Bloomsbury, to Lena's door, Strether kissed Lena's hand, she laughed, kissed Max on his cheek, then Strether accompanied Max to his hotel and set off in the dark.

Max was jealous. Not of Thibault but of Strether.

30

At the Regent they didn't talk only of Mons, sometimes Max told stories about life in London, indiscretions, news items he'd just heard on the agency's telegraphs, he enjoyed having more information than a great maître d'. That is the art of the interview, if you want others to speak to you then you have to speak to them, you have to create a little quid pro quo, an exchange of news, tell what you, yourself, know, and the other will want to outbid you.

41

Max had them a bit on the edges of their seats with a story of a gramophone, a violin and the Lord Chief Justice, a story highly relevant today, they didn't know if Max was serious in saying 'highly relevant', a mother, a late-model gramophone and a violin, the family had reached the lower ranks of the middle class, it was hoping to continue its rise through culture, music for the children, it's very lovely, said Max, until the husband finds himself out of work, and all of a sudden the gramophone and the violin are at the pawnbroker's, a little cash, but the sadness of the children, and the appearance of the Lord Chief Justice, or rather the appearance of the woman before the the Lord Chief Justice, for an assault against the right of the children of the middle class to a musical education? No, but I'll save the rest for tomorrow, ladies and gentlemen, because I have a train to catch early tomorrow, where? Shhh, not a word . . . let's just say Oxford, or Birmingham, I haven't decided yet.

Strether hadn't liked the interruption, nor the allusion to Birmingham.

31

Back from his train excursion the following evening, Max finished his story about a gramophone, a violin and the Lord Chief Justice: if they come together, it's because the gramophone and the violin are only rent-to-own, they don't belong to the woman who pawned them but to a shop-owner legally pursuing the woman for having stopped paying the monthly instalments—that's what being unemployed will get you.

And the Counsel to the Crown says that she committed a true crime, she could even spend a few weeks in prison, a good example to set now when mothers are going to pawnbrokers with just about anything.

The Lord Chief Justice reflects, and decides to be lenient, because, he says, the woman has six children and a good character.

Lena says to Max that he doesn't have to be sarcastic when he tells that story, and Strether adds that the woman did what she did because she couldn't even look for work when her husband lost his job, women shouldn't take men's jobs, and if they are put into prison each time they take a suspicious object to a pawnbroker they would then have to look for work, and that's not good for society.

'Right,' said Lena, looking at Strether, 'then women would risk losing their good character.'

Max wasn't displeased with this little tension between Strether and Lena. And that reminded him how much he hated Thibault.

PART IV

To Break Up or Not to Break Up

32

Eventually Lena and Thibault began to clash less during their rehearsals. 'You're like all couples,' said Max, 'you're smoothing out the rough edges.'

Then Lena decided to break up with Thibault. And not even because of the goat-faced novelist.

It happened one morning, Lena went into a perfume shop but she didn't do what she usually did, or, she first did what she always did, put a small dab on the back of her hand, breathed in. It was afterwards that everything changed, she did not begin to wonder what Thibault's reaction to the perfume might be nor that she would later smell the scent on his skin.

She didn't wonder anything at all, she thought about the perfume, breathed in, nothing more, she wanted something citrusy, lemon leaf, a summer perfume, the saleswoman must think I'm looking for a man's cologne and not daring to ask.

And Lena realized that for such an important purchase she was no longer thinking of her lover, that she no longer wanted to think about him.

She thought about Strether, but that wasn't it. Strether hadn't taken Thibault's place. Lena was incapable of saying why she wasn't attracted to Strether. He was handsome, he had a past, he had stories to tell, and, if he lingered the way he did every night, perhaps even a wife that didn't suit him. But she wasn't attracted to him.

It was as if she had crossed a threshold without realizing it, she no longer raised her head every five minutes while she thought of Thibault, she was once again alone in her own life.

33

The break-up went well, Lena was in full control, with a beautiful coldness, unexpected, Thibault entering the apartment, trying to embrace Lena, Lena pulling away, the kind teacher, 'Thibault, I'd like to tell you . . .' and then, very American, surgical, 'It's over,' a little smile, 'but we'll continue to work together,' Lena cold and reassuring.

Thibault was at a bit of a loss, because it's difficult to feign emotion, pain, sadness, protest, incomprehension, appeal, when your deepest feelings are summed up in one syllable, a 'phew' that you must above all not reveal, to establish sincere feelings off of a 'phew' requires talents beyond those of a little showman, Lena was very satisfied with the friendly coldness she was showing, *I was afraid of myself, you prepare yourself, you assume a look, and suddenly you can't stand up, you sense you're pale, he's there, a few feet away, you put your hand on a side table to hold yourself up, there is sunlight on the table, a nice heat on your hand, you're able to talk, if my vocal chords stay in this condition the rehearsal will be great, we frighten each other, he seems anxious too, that's reassuring, Max was right, Thibault really does look like a gigolo, with his too-pointy shoes, a white jacket, you can't imagine such a jacket, my voice quickly became strong, I didn't tremble, he didn't either, he immediately understood that I wouldn't lower myself to change pianists, that's what he was most worried about.*

Thibault's reaction was minimal, his mouth half-open, for a moment, then, 'I assume nothing will make you change your mind?'

34

The day of the break-up Lena and Thibault had decided to work on the first three lieder, then they began to go over the last one, 'We have to know what we're doing,' Lena had said, the lied of the empty world and the first pain, '*Nun hast du mir den ersten Schmerz getan,* now you have caused my first pain, *Der aber traf,* that which truly hurts, in the poem the man is asleep.' *Thibault is sleeping in the arms of a neurotic novelist, is she really neurotic? Thibault is the neurotic one, to sleep with such a scrawny woman, he is sleeping with a woman who thinks he is intelligent, it's his way of thinking he's intelligent.*

'It's magnificent, *Nun hast du mir*, the simplest words in the best possible order, *nun*, we're still in the present, she has just said "you are my happiness, you are my pleasure" and *nun*, it can still be that, happiness, but Schumann's music already indicates the opposite, it's the pain of a woman in love, and so the first hypothesis one can make while listening to it is that she has been betrayed, a betrayal in love, the first hurt, we have all experienced that.'

And Lena said this, surprised that she could do so with such delicious calm.

She also thought that she should perhaps visit the novelist, dear friend, I know one doesn't speak of such things but I'm not American for nothing, I came to thank you, you have changed him, he has begun to try to think, I find that wonderful, the novelist is taken aback, no, not her style, she looks at me sweetly, she is already sizing me up for a chapter, it's best that I not go, yes, but if she uses Thibault in one of her books I'll be in it too, too bad, in any case novelists don't really like music, when they put music in a book it's music without notes.

And the lied advanced to the highest note, the B flat, on *leer*, the world is empty, *die Welt ist leer*, my B flat, while Thibault, at the piano, has already decided, yes, on dissonance.

35

It's growing dark. Lena is walking down the street with a determined gait, the gait of someone walking a long distance, then she abruptly turns round, she's going in the wrong direction, again with a determined gait, some hundred metres, and another, unexpected, but natural about-face, she does it again at the end of two hundred metres, back and forth, it's the only way not to be accosted, a determined gait, staying under the lights of the street lamps. *What is that scent of flowers? When I was young I could recognize them, hyacinth, reseda, geranium, it must be hyacinths, I'm babbling, I've lost everything living in cities.* At the same time Lena tries to keep an eye on a window on the sixth floor on the other side of the little square, to see without being seen, without looking like a guard on patrol in front of Buckingham Palace. Without being approached, either.

She can't see very much, only that there is light in the window. He's there.

She's been doing this for several days. Some evenings she takes a taxi and has it go round the square and the block of houses, park for a moment, always from where she can see the window. Some drivers are discreet, others take the opportunity to speak to her inappropriately. She gets out and continues her surveillance on foot, this causes people to give strange looks, women aren't supposed to be out alone at night.

36

On the other side of the square is an entrance lit by a harsh light, an awning that appears golden yellow in the glow. *The hotel is pretentious, Thibault wanted his independence, to act respectable, he could have come and lived with me at the Langtons', but no, he needed his own address for his contacts. And for his other women. I expected as much from the beginning. I accepted it. Golden yellow, he could have chosen a less flashy hotel. I wonder what his women think. Maybe the vulgarity excites them.*

It's chilly this evening. Even though it's August. Not as chilly as all that after walking for a while, I must be careful not to catch a cold, not to linger too long, I'll have to leave without knowing anything for sure. Actually, you'll probably catch cold at the Regent bar but there you can't decide to leave early.

The light in the window, he's not the type to stay alone in a hotel room, I shouldn't have broken up with him, he agreed too quickly, now he always comes over with his agent, sometimes with one or two new friends, and I'm friendly, we don't sleep together any more, I avoid conflicts, we are two musicians fulfilling our contracts, a contract that forces me to sing with a mediocre pianist, whom I requested, who will play his maudlin notes while leaning out towards the audience, I know him, he has calmed down during rehearsals, he does it less, but in front of the audience he'll start up again.

And Max has understood everything and he teases me, and I must pretend to beg him to bring me with him when he meets Strether, but Max should be asking me to go with him, I like those evenings with the three of us, with the colonel with delicate hands, he has prejudices but he's quite the gentleman, and he's looking at me more and more.

No shadows behind the curtains, only light, maybe Thibault just forgot to turn out the light before going out, I'm not even sure there is someone, 'This woman is very enchanting, not because she sings but because she likes beer and knows how to have a good time,' that's what Strether said about me.

Abandoned by Thibault, reduced to pacing on the street. That's wrong, I'm the one who left Thibault. I thought it was easy not to love any more, now I'm pacing under his window. And I'm really not attracted to Strether.

37

Lena under Thibault's hotel room window. *After all, he's not the first man I've left, but that's jealousy, waiting under someone's windows, like in a French novel, a man who is not really in love but who becomes so after watching his mistress at night. Were there stars like there are tonight? It's rare to have stars in the London sky, I leave a man and I find myself under his window, and every past pleasure becomes a wound, and Max has understood and offers quotes, it's very French, 'deep in the forest, were they going* to hide?' *for me it's in my drawing room, when the guests have left, and always with the wish to kill the other one, to throw her in the Thames, no, to throw myself in the water, then the man realizes how much he loves me, he leaves the other, he comes to cry over my body that has been pulled from the river.*

It's the novelist who will be happy, a woman with colourless lips, who dares to show such collarbones, she shows the hollows in her collarbones to Thibault, implying to him: I hide nothing from you, you won't have any bad surprises. That's what you call an arrogant flaw.

And for the second time, Lena saw the novelist standing up, in her drawing room in Hampstead, she'd placed her hands on the edge of the table and Thibault passed behind her, *I almost didn't see it but that's it, that's the image.*

At that moment Lena understood everything, *it was like the dolphins, there were elephants embroidered on the novelist's tablecloth, he pointed at them, laughing, I'm sure he was thinking of the dolphins, the ones embroidered on my tablecloth in Paris, and our two champagne glasses, shaking, I saw those dolphins, the mocking eyes of the dolphins on the tablecloth, I was bent over them, and over the champagne glasses, I gripped the edge of the table, he stood behind me and in the mirror in front, to the left, moving and casual, with the suppleness of a dolphin, and I was surprised to cry out as I did, he is also going to do that with her, the casual dolphin, he did it, and I'm sure she added something to her cry, elephants, what an idea, a very leftist novelist with animals that came with the Empire on her tablecloth, a cry of love in front of the elephants of the Indian army, what next?*

38

Lena stopped her guard duty in front of Thibault's hotel. It was stupid, a woman who has a house has no reason to creep round a hotel.

Lena has now taken up her watch in Hampstead, not far from the novelist's house, she is watching the movements of other curtains and she is no longer alone on the street. Max offered to join her. How did he know? He responded that he was in a good position to know that jealousy demanded to know everything.

'You always have to research a story like a jealous person, my dear. The journalist is too often happy with a "probably" or a "one says that . . ." Whereas a jealous person wants a real date, a real word, real accounts, a real report, the jealous person is the reporter par excellence, we're going to go together to watch your little gigolo, I don't want you alone on the street at this hour, you could get into trouble, passion might make a comeback. And I won't ask for anything in return because I'm a normal man, sad and easy.'

Lena hadn't reacted to 'little gigolo', such words were one of Max's pleasures, it didn't matter much and it felt good to say little gigolo, it didn't change much in the situation, she'd always known that Thibault was only a little gigolo, that was probably one of his attractions, someone who wanted her out of self-interest, she had never experienced that, she had only known admirers, devotés, she had thought she would take on a little cynic and make him fall in love.

Of course Max didn't know everything, he was interested only in what could feed his suffering, about which Lena cared little, and so Max ended up accompanying Lena on her nocturnal rounds, he was helping a jealous woman spy on a man worth ten times less than she, he was helping her feed her suffering because she was suffering from the same illness, and he was waiting for what would come next, *we look wonderful, she and I, walking around every night, watching the window of a little gigolo, I assume this'll speed up the end but I have to imagine another scenario, when she'll take the little gigolo back, the pleasures of the reunion, when one resumes the gestures one thought were dead, and the ruined reunion, the second round of indifference, the worst, or the good. I'm an idiot to believe that she'll be grateful to me for helping her with all this, in any case I don't want her gratitude, she breaks up with a guy and then goes crazy with jealousy, then asks another jealous guy to come with her to find proof for her jealousy. I know what I'm getting myself into.*

Then Lena and Max went to meet Strether at the Regent.

39

Max and Lena also talked about Strether and his wife, Lena was the one who wanted to talk about the wife but Max refused, laughing, 'I don't talk about the wives of married men, especially with you. Why? Because you're thinking of the best way you can make that woman disappear,' said Max, 'when you are really done with the little gigolo, and I don't want to be an accomplice to an assassination.' Max was being nice, he assumed Lena had another desire, from the suffering that made them walk in the evenings in Hampstead, looking for useless proof.

To punish Max for his refusal to talk about Mrs Strether, Lena acted surprised at his great interest in the colonel, 'He is, after all, what in France you'd call a complete reactionary, Max, a guy looking for a new war, have you really begun to like those people?' Max hadn't replied.

Lena had decided to pick the scab, she called Max a vengeful war veteran and Max, one evening, stopped, his back to the fence of the little square, he closed his eyes, and began to speak slowly, and Lena waited a few seconds before realizing that he was reciting, 'The war came and took them and they hated their chiefs and obeyed orders and killed each other. And it's all forgotten. They'll be taken again and hate their chiefs again and obey orders again and—kill each other. Again and again. That's what people are. They might be different if they wanted to. But they don't want to. They mock life. They scourge and spit upon and crucify life. Again and again and for ever.'

'Who wrote that, Max?'

'Toller, my dear, Ernst Toller, a play, *Hinkemann*, a bit strong, isn't it? And it's my entire generation, everywhere in Europe, but quiet! Not a word! And you know what those cretins in black or brown shirts will do? They're going to persuade me that it'll soon be necessary to go back to war, against them, and I told you about my young friend, the guy who was caught a few years ago taking a couple of statuettes from Angkor, who started an anti-colonialist paper in Saigon? He's becoming a good novelist with stories about Asia, he thinks the next war has already begun in China, in Shanghai, Hankow, he says that what follows will only be a shifting of the front to the West.'

40

In the end, Max did not understand Lena's behaviour, those vigils under the windows, he didn't recognize her, she had more character than that, she was the sort to threaten the novelist with throwing her down the stairs if she didn't break things off immediately with Thibault, whereas here she was showing hesitation, complacency in her pain shared with good company.

One evening, while they were strolling, Max had a revelation, he needed to stay silent to begin to believe what he had just realized. But Lena provoked him, 'You're as silent as someone who's got a juicy titbit. It's wrong not to tell your friend.'

'That's enough,' Max exploded, 'I get it, this thing isn't working, it will never work. We're stopping. We're leaving.'

'What do you get, Max? That you have other things to do with your time than to help a friend who's going through a fit of jealousy?'

'This will never work, you're not jealous!'

Lena stood immobile in the shadows, silent.

'You don't love him, you're not in love!'

'So it's for the pleasure of your company that I'm walking around here?'

'You don't feel anything, Lena, that's what's making you ill to the point of walking under the windows, but this won't ignite anything in you at all.'

Max looked at her. Between the shadows and the light.

'You know what's going on here? It's a thirty-five-year-old crisis, that's all. Since you're American you're trying to find an empirical remedy—for every problem there's a solution, so you walk under the windows of this novelist, so it will all come back, so you walk to make desire be reborn, every night! If a lack of desire pushes you to keep watch under windows, you must, as if it's enough to keep watch under windows to make desire return! I almost pitied you, you got rid of your desire for a man,' Max pointed at the end of the street, 'and you saw desire itself go away, that's what really frightens you!

'Come on, you'll get over it, at your age the sadness in the body doesn't last, ciao Rubato, let's go to the Regent, Strether talks a lot better when you're there, I need you, and it's not love, it's serious.'

41

Lena didn't return to the windows of the Hampstead house. She wasn't very happy with what she'd gone through with Thibault. She consoled herself sometimes by thinking that in love as in rehearsals you had to make every mistake.

Just before their first recital, Thibault, who had become an acceptable accompanist, asked her what she hoped to achieve. He was frustrated by the 'absence of expression' which Lena insisted on.

'What I'm seeking is the secret fibre,' she replied.

'In the end,' said Thibault, 'we're looking for the same thing.'

He hadn't added that he thought it was futile to have clashed to such a degree. And Lena did not think it wise to explain to him that they weren't looking for the same thing at all, that her secret fibre came from Nerval, when he spoke of Schumann, of the *Dichterliebe*, a music that *touches the secret fibre*. For Nerval, the fibre doesn't exist before the music, it's not a fibre hidden in a person and that is awakened by the music, it's a fibre that exists only for the duration of the work, that disappears with it, that must constantly be created anew.

Lena didn't say a thing to Thibault about Nerval's ideas, because he wouldn't have been able to tell them to his goat-faced novelist without hacking them to pieces.

PART V

An Outstretched Hand

42

One night, walking Max back to his hotel, Strether said, 'The soldiers didn't see angels, it was superstition, or because at a certain point in battle the men are so ensconced in the inhuman that they become angels, it isn't angels who come to help the men but the men themselves who must lose their earthly faculties that prevent them from fighting well, men who are trans-formed into angels of war.'

Strether was repeating himself, droning on, although he'd had only a beer and a whisky.

'. . . at night, Max, the din of the German infantry, a night attack, tactical madness, no one had anticipated such a thing, and that's why it worked, a night attack is risky, everyone can get mixed up, you fire on anyone, it works only on one condition, if it instils panic in those you are attacking, they run away, the attackers have only to advance, shooting in front of them, with a rocket blast from time to time.

'Max, what the Germans saw . . . By the way, how was your trip the other day? You mentioned Birmingham, I think, oh, it doesn't matter, forgive my indiscretion, Max, what the Germans saw—'

Strether is under a street lamp, his clean-shaven, delicate face, the light casts shadows under his eyes and nose.

'—what they really saw in front of them was not angels but the archers of Azincourt!'

43

In front of his hotel Max looked at Strether while trying not to show that he thought him mad. Strether continued in his soft, hoarse voice, adding that at Azincourt, already, King Arthur and some knights of the Round Table had intervened on behalf of the English. It was a great cycle, Max should understand, it was time.

'You well know, Max, time isn't simple, it winds round, it backtracks, a straight line for time is an invention of the papists and communists, Max, there are recesses in the flow of time, and hidden in those recesses is a knighthood, immortal, always ready to surge forth, to be reincarnated when History is sliding off track, today it's time for the knights to stand up, knights like those archers at Mons, like Lancelot, Tristan and King Arthur at Azincourt, like the Teutonic knights in the East, like here right now, in the face of those Reds on strike.'

Max thought that Strether was mixing up chivalry with the archers but it wasn't the moment to contradict him.

'I know, Max, you're going to criticize me for being a Fascist, you don't like that, like all the friends of the Reds, you sympathize with the Reds, right? Come on, just a bit? Like all the people in the newspaper business, and many of the French, but I also know that you would never ignore an opportunity to understand the other side, a knighthood, Max, that comes from the recesses of time, today in England there are men who have responded to the call, who have resumed the mission, as elsewhere in Europe, who have succeeded in Italy, who will succeed in Germany, in France, Max, with the support of those who came to help us in Mons, the archers, don't laugh, the intangible archers, from the recesses of time.'

45

'Max,' said Strether under the street lamp, 'those intangible archers, I am not so stupid as to believe that I could have touched them, they are untouched.'

Max tried to keep a straight face, Strether sounded like one of those sidewalk swindlers who promise salvation or hell while an accomplice picks your pocket.

'Untouched, Max, but whom, during the night at Mons, we believed to be as hard as iron, and it is thanks to that that we were able to retreat in an orderly fashion, you understand? And that orderly retreat, thanks to the archers, while our actual leaders were in a dream state,

HÉDI KADDOUR

that masterly retreat, that was reality, you understand, Max, those intangible archers, they created a reality, that is what they are good for, angels, archers, knights, to create reality, and in Italy it's not archers but legionnaires, the tenth legion of Caesar, his veterans, those who saved him in Pharsalus, who returned to sweep away the Reds, who entered Rome with Mussolini, Max, compared to real results the question of the reality of the knights is secondary.'

Strether was gripping Max's arm and didn't realize he was hurting him.

45

Max thought Strether was crazy, a crazy person who believed in the return of the archers of Azincourt, hiding in the recesses of history. And that madness deserved a story.

He was going to be able to write a sensational piece rather than just the simple story of a reserve officer tempted by the extreme Right.

At one point he realized that Strether did not really want to go any further. Which meant that there was probably more to the story, a secret, perhaps. He tried to look entranced with Strether's explanations of the recesses of history, to the point of looking like he believed what he was being told. But that wasn't enough, Strether was repeating himself, again, offering no more names of people or places, no longer wanting to open Pandora's box.

And so Max changed tactics, asked that they get to the heart of the subject, those stories of the veterans, of angels, of battles, of knights, that was fine for a time but he would now like to talk about the present.

'That's my profession, dear Colonel, current affairs, I'm not a historian or a novelist, I work on what's going on at this moment, in Europe and in London, on what makes headlines, even on page four or five, upheaval in poor neighbourhoods, what's happening in the Conservative Party, in the Chamber of Lords, among certain members of the Labour Party, I know a very conservative Lord Raglan but he speaks of you as a canker, it's not very nice, you're really trying to overturn them, the upper crust? My boss is really going to like these sorts of things.'

46

Max had decided to shake Strether up a little.

'And we should begin with the beginning, Colonel. Your comings and goings, your little bits of the past in the present, the spiralling speeches that return to the same points while embellishing them, that's prose for artists or for bar clients, but my readers and I want a true beginning, how did this all begin for you? How does one become a Fascist?'

Max added that, thanks to his report, the party, its truths, its ambitions, were going to reach a European audience and, in the competition between English Fascists, that would be important, this story would be in a large French newspaper.

'But you're going to have to give me some facts, Colonel.'

Strether didn't say a word, his look implored Lena to speak up but she refrained from saying anything. It was amusing to see him in the hot seat, required to respond to questions other than those he had expected not to answer. He didn't seem to like his past.

In fact, Strether was exactly where Max wanted him—he was going to respond with reticence to the questions that were not so indiscreet and do all he could to continue telling his tall tales of angels and archers, suggesting the existence of groups more influential than those which paraded behind him in public. He just needed a bit more time.

47

'There's no lack of Fascist parties here,' Max said to Lena, while walking with her over Tower Bridge, 'they all dream of repeating what Mussolini did. You start with a handful and one day, after a few demonstrations, you have it all, and the smaller the initial handful the greater the success, it creates lots of ambition, the Imperial

Fascist League, the British Empire Fascists, the Fascist League, even the Green Shirt Movement for Social Credit and the Yorkshire Fascists, I'll refrain from giving you the entire list but there are a lot of people who work against each other, a true hornet's nest.

'Strether could really give me all the background on that but he fears being swallowed up in an in-depth report on him. He'd like to be an anonymous source or even several sources. That's not what I want, there's something more important—he was cagey when he mentioned certain circles not far from power, that's where there should be something meaty.

'You know, my relationship with this guy's strange. I represent what he hates, and he tells me ten times more than he would one of his compatriots, as if a part of him had more things to confide in me than in an Englishman. There are moments when I have the impression that I've become his notary, that one day or another he is going to dictate his will to me.'

48

Strether had finally replied to Max's questions, 'Because of a mailbox, Max. You wanted to know how I joined the party? Because of a mailbox, because I lived in a building with only one mailbox, and one day a neighbour saw an envelope addressed to Colonel William Strether, DSO. That neighbour was a veteran too, we spoke, he'd been a hundred kilometres from Mons at the time of the battle, he was a bit jealous of me, he introduced himself, we got on. He was, and still is, a member of the British Fascist League, he invited me to a meeting.

'Do you know what I found there, Max? Not conservatives, not demagogues, not failures, but people who wanted to change society, with order, and who knew where the enemy was, like we had in 1914, that's why we went, for the hope of a new world, but with order, that's what I liked, the Fascist League gave me back the feeling of a group, yes, while looking for work I had lost that a bit, the concerns of a group, of the country, of the future, a reserve colonel like me could mean something in a party like that.

'I didn't have a job, Max, I couldn't find one, and what was worse were the people who apologized for not being able to offer me the ones that were available, they were ashamed to hire a colonel to sort the mail.

'Their president wanted to see me, he quickly understood that I was in difficulty, he proposed that I manage his office, he didn't say that to me exactly, he said he needed a confidential collaborator.

'I had a wife to feed, I began by sorting his mail, at the bottom of the ladder, employed by a man who was also ashamed to give me such tasks but who paid me a small salary, I considered it a beginning. Then I began to organize the president's office, his files, a bit.'

49

'I was well aware,' Strether told Max, 'that this work with the League's president was beneath me but I stuck with it, those people had held out their hand to me, and the president asked me to take on more and more. Don't write this, Max, but people who speak of order don't really know what it is, especially on a day-to-day level. As for me, if I'm assigned a task, then two, three days later it's done, and in order, and that's how I advanced. You can say in your articles that I was on the dole, that I was often forced to join the soup line. There was no shame in that,' Strether added, looking at Lena. Max hadn't blinked when Strether had said 'your articles,' and Strether had come to the conclusion that the story would be developed over several instalments. That gave him more energy.

Max wasn't content with Strether's confidences alone. He also questioned other members of the party. His admirers. They all spoke of Strether's calm.

Max dug around. He found people who'd left the party, who spoke of Strether in a different way, a disturbing man, too reserved, no one ever heard him burst out laughing, he didn't drink enough when they went out together, he rarely spoke in public, took no defined position, he waited for when he was alone with the leaders. The model of the boot-licker, not virile enough to be honest, said all those who had left the British Fascist League. Max thought they were rather bitter.

50

Very quickly Strether became a most trustworthy secretary, and more, an office manager, without the title,
nor really the salary, but with the power, the guy who
arrives on time, who writes without making mistakes,
who prioritizes duties, keeps accounts, prepares the
meeting agendas. He also knew how to forget what
shouldn't be repeated.

Strether had put on the beret and the black shirt,
he had marched with the party. Often, due to war
wounds, he was forced to use a cane.

He did even better. One day, returning from a
League meeting, the president was attacked by three
men, Reds, he was with Strether, Strether held the men
off with his cane, he was a specialist in cane-fighting,
not very forceful but precise, his opponent expects to
receive a blow to his head, he anticipates parries, takes
a bad blow to his knee cap, calculated blows, vicious,
that's what the injured men said at the police station.

And so the president asked Strether to train the
young men in the party's security forces. That didn't
please the leader of those forces, but he drank too much.
The president replaced him with Strether, Strether
refused, the president went above him and paid him a
bonus for the new position.

Strether had to learn that new profession very
quickly, a security force is not just cane-fighting. But,

since it was not that different from a military function, he figured it out, he listened to the section heads, those with experience, who had a lot of respect for a veteran of Mons. Listening on the one hand, respect on the other, they had done away with disorder and surprises. Strether introduced caution. He commanded little, anticipated a lot. It worked. The party leaders were happy, and Strether had almost become one of them.

PART VI

A Sentimental Education

51

One morning, Max and Lena were strolling along West-minster Bridge, taking advantage of the cool morning air. They ran into Strether, and Strether introduced them to his wife. He said only 'my wife', not her name. She was rather tall, with grey eyes, she was reserved, spoke little. Lena thought she was holding her purse awkwardly, that she looked more like the wife of a puritan minister than of a military officer.

She exuded the sadness of those who have wasted their lives.

Later, at the end of the story, when Max had learnt everything, he said on many occasions that the true beginning was not the parade of 1930. The parade was only an apparent display of order, the story of a man, a veil of order. The truth was more chaotic.

Everything had begun much earlier, with the encounter of a woman and an officer, at the beginning of the war. There was an outing in the country. The officer had returned from France, he was on leave. 'A lovely country outing,' said Max, 'which we love to talk about by trying to put ourselves alongside the one who loved it the most.'

52

She remembers leafy trees and the banks of a lake. He called her 'my tall one,' she thought that was funny. It was a Sunday. And yet she hadn't planned to go out. Sitting in an armchair, her nail file in her hand, she was tackling her nails. She didn't say to herself that she would end up reading stupid magazines or playing solitaire, because those are things one doesn't say to oneself, you know you're going to end up doing them but you don't get up in the morning and say, 'Today I'm going to play solitaire.' Cards are what remains when the day is dead, and one prefers to have other desires when one wakes up, hopes, even. One passes the day dropping them one by one.

She might have had an encouraging phone call, Cedric, for example, the boy who promised to call her back, a good-looking boy, with a car that seemed to belong to him, but no, he wouldn't call, *don't think about it, my dear, you're at the bottom of the heap, even if you are much more refined than your peers.*

She hadn't thought about it but she had in fact received a phone call from a married friend, Virginia, who had invited her to an outing in the country. She had refused, it felt like a last-minute fix-up, *tell your friend I have nothing against him, it's just that I'm not a lifesaver, no Virginia, I'm not angry at you, you're sweet, but I'm not coming, no, you can't resist the idea of doing good even when you know you're going to hurt someone, or maybe you want to hurt me? No, that's not what I meant, I don't think that, but you know that by insisting you're hurting me.*

She had hung up. Too bad, Virginia was going to explode and say, 'I'll never understand Gladys, she's becoming even touchier, but she needs a boyfriend, she can't stay like that, and when you offer her one, she sends you packing.' And she heard another commentary, the voice of Oscar, Virginia's husband, something like, 'Yes, Gladys really should make an effort,' which really meant that she was no beauty queen.

53

It was Virginia and Oscar's friend who called Gladys a moment later, 'I won't be a problem, I'm leaving for the front tomorrow.' She was angry for a moment at what seemed to her to be emotional blackmail, then she agreed to go with them.

They met at the train station, in the hubbub of a joyful crowd, people jostling along the platform. It was an autumn morning, the beginning of autumn, when the fruit is ripe and the sun is reluctant to abandon the heat of summer. Shortly after their train pulled out, the branches of still-leafy trees began to gaily beat against the windows of their car, they felt like singing, and the light cast beams upon their faces and forearms. The train followed a little road where they sometimes saw a truck bouncing along under sacks of grain or a hay wagon whose upper layers of its burden were picked off by the trees.

In the end, the friend wasn't too bad, at least he spoke slowly, wanting to be heard, a rather tall lieutenant in civilian clothes. The train wasn't going very fast, it chugged along noisily, whistling every four or five hundred yards, as if it were watching for any bad surprises along the way. It stopped often, in stations with red roofs that resembled dolls' houses placed along the tracks, and on the platforms, baskets of fruit and casks of milk waited for the train that would come from the opposite direction and go back to London. Once they had even stopped in what could only be called a farmyard. It smelt of hay, stables, the summer, the city seemed aeons behind them. The war, too.

Gladys talked with the three others while remembering her childhood in the country. It was lovely.

54

The train ride through the countryside lasted about an hour, Gladys felt much more comfortable, even if it wasn't easy to talk with someone she didn't know when a couple who had been married for several years took it upon themselves to encourage the conversation.

When they went out with other people Virginia had the habit of saying 'Gladys is a girl with many talents,' or 'Everyone knows that your still waters run deep.' Try to talk naturally with a man you have just met when your friend says such things. And her husband, though not saying anything like that, did nothing to prevent his wife, which made him even more obnoxious than a simple boor, because his wife thus emphasized her words with his silence, a silence that made it seem that they knew even more than they were divulging. But that day Virginia and Oscar were perfect.

They had got out at the edge of a forest, they had walked in the warmth of the sun, under the oak trees, the pines, the beeches, each carrying a picnic basket and the friend a rather heavy suitcase. 'It's a surprise,' was all he'd said. They had let him keep his secret though they thought they knew what it was.

He had light eyes, long hands, he hadn't said what he was doing in the war, she hadn't asked.

55

On the day of the outing, Gladys was wearing a wide-brimmed straw hat with a little white feather, very stylish, and she was cursing her shoes, they enhanced her calves but made her look like a big chicken when she walked on the sand of the path. And she preferred not to think of her dress, ill-suited to hide what she was, a beanpole, with bones, skin, big steps, the cliché of the English woman, even if she had been lucky and didn't have the large teeth that usually went with the cliché. The lieutenant knew how to offer his hand to help her across a ditch and then to seem to forget his gesture. After a half-hour walk they decided to stop alongside a lake.

They talked, seated on a large blanket, talked about everything, very little about what was going on over there on the continent. Virginia's husband was not in the military, his profession had spared him a departure to the front, a bit of luck, you might say, he was an explosives specialist. That's all he said. From time to time a silence interrupted the conversation and they all watched the last swallows of the season flying on the surface of the water, piercing through the clouds of gnats.

They talked about jams, cooking, welcoming little towns, memories of outings, childhood. Out of a spirit of contradiction she lavished praise on London, she quoted something she had read in a book that she had liked, 'The air of big cities makes you free.' Oscar and Virginia looked at each other—just the thing to say if you are a woman talking to an officer!

56

After a while the two men left the banks of the water and slipped into the woods. Gladys took advantage of their absence to remark to Virgina, 'How could this lieutenant have been able to go on leave so soon after the beginning of the war?' He didn't look like a noble-man's son. Virginia had heard that he did other things, that it was a leave for bravery in the line of duty, that he was the type of officer a war could promote rather quickly to a higher grade, if he survived.

The two men returned wearing large, white bathing suits with navy blue stripes. They dived in, splashed, laughed. She and Virginia, still seated, watched them, laughing too, happy to have a pretext for staring at their companions. It was hot. They felt increasingly stifled in their dresses.

Virginia took Gladys by the hand and they in turn disappeared into the woods. Gladys had to help Virginia pin up the skirt of her bathing suit, and they returned to swim with the men. She had happily taken off her shoes, not minding the discomfort of the gravel which made Virginia cry out.

'You swim well,' the friend told her. 'I was raised in the country,' she had replied, 'with boys.' All four of them played in the water, and got along famously.

57

After they finished swimming the lieutenant opened his suitcase. They danced in their swimming suits on the sand, to the music from his gramophone. They got dressed, lunched on chicken pâté, roast pork en gelée, quite fatty, with enough salt so that they eagerly drank more beer, then pudding, and coffee that tasted like the thermos. During the meal the lieutenant dared to call Gladys by her first name rather than Miss Walthers. Then Virginia's husband asked permission to take a little nap. Gladys had taken Virginia's arm, saying, 'The only thing more naturally beautiful than a drunk man is a man who snores!'

When he woke up they set off on a hike. The men ran, they found a little dead tree stump that they threw to each other like a rugby ball. They also found things to pick up, a bottle, a porcelain bowl, a packet of Players, they made up stories for them, exotic adventures, laughing, sometimes jumping over a winding stream that they were following without realizing it. Virginia threw the lieutenant's cap up in the air, the cap got stuck in a tree. Gladys climbed up to get it. The men complimented her. She also impressed them with her way of finding her way in the middle of the woods, of distinguishing between the rustling of a field mouse and the slithering of a grass snake, 'No, vipers are rare and you don't hear them coming,' she said to frighten Virginia.

58

Then, in the middle of the woods, Gladys asked her three friends to take a detour, she heard before anyone else the sound of bees at work, 'Let's not get too close, it's their territory, the nest must be in a stump a bit farther, can you smell the wild honey?' They sniffed, and agreed, with good humour.

Farther, without warning, Virginia and her husband disappeared, leaving her alone with the lieutenant. She continued to walk with him, not speaking. Then they lay down side by side, watching the clouds. He spoke kindly. He had studied law and was hesitating between a military or civilian life, when the war was over, of course. After a moment she rolled over against him.

Shortly before five o'clock they all met at the lake. Each couple had a boat. It touched her to see him sitting in front of her as if they had been together for ever. She didn't try to think. And nothing in her sought to reject that man, that was new. Maybe she was happy. She didn't really know. Two young girls passed them in another boat, he responded with laughter to their greeting, she hated them. Then sudden tenderness flowed through her again. He watched her, smiling.

He left the next morning for France, returning two months later thanks to another leave for bravery. They got married.

She was happy and ill at ease, he was serious. He told her he felt increasingly fragile and that he loved her because he found her robust and bold. He called her 'my tall one' and treated her as an equal, he knew almost as many Dickens' novels as she did but not the Brontë sisters. She sent him books and forbade him from seeking leaves for bravery.

Yet he did come back more often than others. Then one day he did not.

The Ministry of War regrets to inform you . . . etc.

59

Gladys found herself the widow of a decorated man. She would start crying at any moment of the day, falling onto a chair, into any available corner.

And so she set off to join the war, driving ambulances, sometimes under shell fire, holding the hands of the dying among the smell of bleach and wounds that almost never healed. She did this for a year and a half, and was awarded one of the special medals created just for women. She also experienced feverish evenings, when men going back to the front looked at her in a bar, smiling. She often did what the other female ambulance drivers did, but she never got used to desire without love.

Then she returned to England. It was the time the suffragettes called on women to support the war effort by working in factories rather than by knitting or baking cakes.

She preferred working in a factory. She was assigned to a locomotive factory converted into a factory for planes, tanks, explosives, artificial limbs. There were two sites, each baptized in honour of a war, *Marne* and *Mons*.

She began working in *Mons*, with the 'canaries'. That was the name given to the women who made TNT—they ended up with yellow skin. It was so dangerous that you didn't work there more than six months. At the end of that time she went on to make airplane wings.

At the end of 1916 there were only women left in her sector, they were housed next to the factory. They worked eight-hour shifts, for less than thirty shillings a week. There was sometimes tension with the union that asserted that women should only be given subaltern tasks in order to protect the salaries and the positions of the men when they returned. Many women had become true professional workers. Merely to avoid any conflict, so they said, the bosses paid them as if they weren't.

60

In 1918, the women had to give everything back to the men. They had a good-bye party and left, crying for the sheet-metal factory or a clothing workshop they had previously cursed every day.

For Gladys, that had at first been a rather pleasant time. The management of the company had called her back to ask if she would serve as a model for one of the panels of a large commemorative window. It was a triptych, with a soldier in the centre, a Tommy alongside Mars, God of War. On the left stood a welder making a sword, she would be on the right, making a shell, in front of a tower, with a helmet on her head.

She wasn't paid for these sessions, she received a small fee but it was unrelated to the cachet of being a model. She never mentioned it. One day, the manager of the factory came to the workshop where she was posing and said to her, 'We chose you because of your bearing, you're tall, you have class, you're a real presence, there's a serious air about you.' He had said *serious* and had interrupted himself after that word, to stress the allusion to her widowhood, to emphasize the memory of the hero who had died for King and Country, that's what her seriousness meant, she had to be alone in front of the machine but one also had to sense in her a mourning for a masculine presence. Those were the manager's exact words: *a mourning for a masculine presence.* 'You're proud to be on this panel, aren't you?' She had understood that, in that man's mind, that more than compensated for the amount she wasn't being paid.

Gladys' parents were dead. She sold their house in Dorset, slowly went through their savings and those she had accumulated when she was on the front and in the factory.

At the beginning of the 1920s she had only her pension to live on, a ridiculous sum that melted away with the rise in prices. She once again began to look for work but it wasn't very seemly for a woman, it meant she didn't have a man.

She needed to become a housewife again, and thus to have a man again, and one wasn't supposed to appear to be looking for a man at a time when there were far fewer than before the war. The women who had one kept you at a distance. Virginia was an exception, but, because of the post-war crash, she and her husband had ended up leaving England and moving to Rhodesia. There was some talk of her joining them. Then the letters came less and less frequently.

61

Then Gladys met another man. His name was Mark, he, too, had been at the front, in France, for close to four years, a survivor. Unlike her husband, he spoke a great deal about it, she listened to his complicated stories. She sensed that he must not have had a role as important as he claimed, nor have known as many specific things about operations, but she was struck by the way he could capture everyone's attention by describing all the battles, it was impressive. She ended up being interested in him, she even surprised herself when she asked him details about such and such an event, when she sometimes corrected some minor point before his audience.

He wasn't bad-looking, or stupid, but she didn't really respect him. He had proposed somewhat awkwardly at the end of a day spent at the seashore. They had gambled, neither winning or losing, then walked out to the end of the pier, it was dark, she knew she should not accept but she told herself she would never have another opportunity. He was skinny, bony, not very tall, with bowed legs. He made up for it with expansive gestures, waving his arms and saying 'I want . . .' with a very convincing air.

Mark raised dogs, Great Danes, chateau dogs. Gladys went to live with him in Kent, freeing Mark's sister who went back to Liverpool.

The brood included eight females. The males were brought by their various owners who left them for a few days with a chosen bitch. The litters were sold, Gladys and Mark managed to live off the business.

She got along very well with the dogs, they weren't at all aggressive. In the evening she'd walk along their cages, in the yard, and large shadows would slip through the dark, looking for a pat on the nose through the fence.

The people who came to buy the dogs all had cars. They were often condescending but they spared no expense.

62

She and Mark soon began to argue, increasingly heatedly, because Mark wanted complete harmony between them. As soon as she was out of sorts, silent, she had to explain herself. She was not allowed to be sombre or silent when he came home very late from an evening with his veteran friends. She didn't like those men, most of them heavy drinkers, 'I know why you're pouting,' he said, no, she wasn't pouting, 'Yes, you think I'm drunk, but it isn't true, you should be ashamed to suspect me, a half-dozen beers, a few whiskies, a bit of gin, I drink just what I need to be at ease with my pals, I'm not an alcoholic.'

He wouldn't sleep until they had finally made up, that is, when she had given in, otherwise he kept her awake or woke her up to pursue the discussion in the dark, he couldn't stand it when she slept and he couldn't. This most often ended in an energetic and fruitless coupling.

She became increasingly unhappy with this man's disorder, his dreams of fortune which he himself didn't believe, his ability to want everything, to do nothing, to imagine that time would solve it all. She found that he spoke to other women in a way that was not that of a married man. She realized that when a woman spoke to him he hardly listened to her, what interested him were the movements of her mouth.

One day, seated in his armchair, his newspaper in his hands, while she was busy in the kitchen, he said to her, 'You think you're so different?' She hadn't responded, he thought he'd had the final word, but that issue of difference had bothered her and she finally understood that Mark was only a false husband to her.

63

After each scene with Mark she promised herself she would divorce him, she didn't want to be one of those women who kept a husband only to argue with him, she liked even less the role into which she all too often fell, that of the wife who gives up, who never reveals her feelings, who tucks her feet under the chair while the man sets out arguments that turn her into a monster.

But she always ended up falling back on what one calls good sense, she scolded herself, told herself she was being unfair.

All they had to do was take a brisk walk, laughing, to once again find the desire to go home together, with the dogs that cavorted round them. Mark had suffered, the war had produced a generation of difficult men, she had to accept that, as she would have accepted a wounded man, it was an infirmity, a war wound. Mark had only to pay her a little attention for her to justify her life again, for her to love him again. He listened to her, she became indulgent and malleable again.

She had become very fond of a large black dog, Betsy. When Betsy ran in the countryside she could out-run a rabbit at a full run. She was aggressive, could hold her own in bloody encounters with another female in the group. But she had no equal in her ability to sense when her mistress wasn't feeling well, at those times she didn't leave her side. She would stay for hours, her head resting on Gladys' shoulder when she was seated, working on the books. Mark sometimes made fun of her, said they looked like an old married couple.

One day a young man had come to buy a puppy. He was in a luxury car, a Bentley with a chauffeur. Betsy had barked at him furiously, he had looked at her, asked that they open the cage, it was dangerous, an accident could ruin their business, but they opened it, and Betsy had thrown her two front paws on the young man's shoulders while he spoke to her in baby-talk.

Mark sold her to him for three times the going price while he whispered to his wife, 'You'll love another one, won't you?'

After the dog was sold, she began to no longer find excuses for Mark's defects and dalliances, she longed for a tall man and Mark no longer attempted to hide Hermione from her.

They divorced. She returned to London where a former co-worker at the factory who was in theatre introduced her to a stage manager. She was hired to do various tasks in the theatre.

PART VII

The Maturing of a Leader

64

Colonel Strether was very much liked by the members of the security forces of the British Fascist League. They competed to see who would be the first to spot him and to shout out the command that pulled everyone to attention. One sensed that he walked with a cohort of illustrious dead behind him.

He had the ability to speak to the young about everything, politics, war, Europe, and, later in the evening, about women. He told them things that the young men didn't dare ask at home. And he knew more than the sharpest among them. He knew better. They sensed that he had lived. But he had settled down, said the members of the party who'd run into him on the street with a woman on his arm, always the same one, shy and silent. Sad, some said. Dignified, said others.

There was a wisdom to Strether. He advised the young men to stay away from women, 'Gold-diggers, they have the feelings of gold-diggers, therefore no feelings at all, but if you want to frequent them, don't lie to them,' he said, 'they'll know it right away, and avoid mystics.' 'What's a mystic, sir?' 'A woman who opens her eyes too wide in front of you, you can tell right away, you think she admires you, but when she widens her eyes it's because you're about to become the solution to her life. And it is very bad to be the solution to a woman's life.'

But he didn't linger on the subject, and those who had met him in the company of his sad-looking wife wondered if it wasn't in fact his own marriage he was talking about.

He sometimes said things that indicated that his ideas on the subject were stronger and more virile than he let on. One of Strether's sayings had even acquired a certain fame, at least in the security forces, 'Above all, don't be bothered by the bad eggs.'

Twice a week, Strether gathered the young men of the security forces and gave them a French cane-fighting lesson. He was not as strong as his height suggested, his leg, his wounds bothered him but he had a quick wrist, arm and hip, and his effectiveness came above all from his look. And he anticipated. He had a lot of presence, with his padded vest, his shoulders thrust back, his left hand behind his back, his movements were fluid, the *brisé*, the *enlevé*, the *croisé tête*, the *croisé bas*.

65

In the weapons room Strether moved with singular grace, he repeated to those who attempted to overcome with strength, 'It is not the grip that influences the trajectory, don't strike with the hand or the forearm.' He placed himself en garde, threw his elbow back, 'From this moment, everything happens with the hip.' The students tried to throw their hips forward, it made Strether smile, 'The hip, young men, should be used as in love, it is a passing zone, not an end,' he bent his legs a bit, 'What are the most powerful muscles in the body?' he straightened his legs, bent them again, 'The thighs, gentlemen, the thighs,' he raised his voice, 'You should learn what is most difficult and most effective—transmit the energy of your thighs to your cane! A blow that comes from the thighs causes ten times more pain than any other!'

There were still more difficult lessons, and Strether constantly stressed them, 'In a training room, the rule is to always parry before lunging, like in sword-fighting, and here you are accustomed to having an opponent who parries before trying to strike you, but on the street it doesn't always work like that, be very careful when you attack, because, even if you make contact, your opponent can strike you at the same time without having attempted to parry,' Strether paused, looked round, 'I have seen men have an eye put out in a simultaneous attack.'

At electoral meetings things always went well when Strether supervised. One, two, several dissenters began to stir up trouble, and Strether walked up to them, accompanied by staunch militants, always more numerous than the dissenters, it was enough to make them leave. Of course, there were insults, but Strether said one shouldn't allow oneself to be provoked by the insults of someone in retreat, one should always leave that exit, the powerless insult, open, and watch the movements, there is always someone who throws something as he leaves, a stick, other objects . . .

'That's what you have to watch out for, my friends, not your little self-esteem.'

Silence.

Strether looked at the faces turned towards him, and continued, 'That little self-esteem always ready to surge forth when one accuses your body of indulging in illicit practices.'

The young men laughed. The leaders of the party appreciated Strether.

There was something else that made him essential—he got along well with the police, to the point that they often allowed Strether's men to finish some of their work with the Reds before intervening. It was said that Strether negotiated man-to-man with the police.

66

Max was calm—he was following the two threads of Strether's story, the angels on the one hand, the party on the other, all he had to do was weave them together and from time to time insert Strether's thoughts on the role of the British Empire in the world, on the dividing up that would be done, 'Eastern Europe to the Aryans of Germany, Southern Europe to the heirs of Caesar, the Middle East and Asia for the most part to those who had them now, that is us, dear Max,' and Max asked 'What about France, dear Colonel?' 'It has Africa,' Strether replied, smiling. One evening he even brought along a world map over which to share his ideas with Max.

And to encourage Strether to speak, Max possessed a decisive weapon—Lena. He used her to push his interlocutor, knowing that the colonel would never want to seem to retreat in the presence of a woman, 'And do you agree with your party's economic policy? Its rather harsh, pure and hard liberalism?' Strether saw the attack coming, didn't react. 'You let the market heal the market,' Max continued, 'with all those people in the soup lines?'

Strether said that one had to stay the course.

'There are no more liberals, Max, there are only stunned politicians.'

Strether's wife never joined them. They met her again on her husband's arm, in the same neighbourhood, but Strether did not attempt to be more sociable.

'You know who she reminds me of?' Max said to Lena, 'An Emma who would have survived, who swallows the poison of married life in small doses. Mme Strether married the wrong man.'

'That's nice, Max, to make literary allusions in front of a poor uncultured American woman. Do you really think that woman looks like she reads books?'

67

Once he got going, Strether had a tendency to want to explain everything about his party, its programme, but Max really didn't want to transform his article into a 'treatise'.

'This is a report-interview that we are doing, dear Colonel, not an off-putting tract, you understand? In a newspaper, each article must fight against the article next to it and on the following page and on the pages of every other newspaper. Battling against boredom is also a true war.'

And each time Strether regressed, Max began to fight against the movements of his lower jaw.

Strether laughed, relaxed, and Max seized the opening, 'Why don't you tell me the story of the boxer?'

Strether wasn't too disconcerted. He knew that Max had been digging, had been collecting gossip. It was best to be a good sport.

'I would prefer to tell that story in front of your friend, Miss Hellström, she doesn't mind somewhat risqué stories, does she? That's a huge part of her charm.'

Max didn't want to discuss Lena's charm with Strether, he requested the story then and there.

'It's an aristocratic story, Max, but you mustn't take that as a severe condemnation of our leading milieu, it was the son of a lord, a duke and a lord, who was to receive those two titles one day or another, he was a member of our security force, very solid, a true boxer, he participated in bare-fisted championships under a pseudonym, I had to constantly keep an eye on him, he was violent. The father was very proud to see his son involved in our defence of true values, and yet one day he wanted to sue the party, we didn't really understand why, he spoke of a gang, the president was very upset.

'He understood when the lord said to him: "In our circle, that's not how you catch syphilis." And he said many generally negative things about the party. The president asked me to speak to him. I had a long conversation with him, his legitimate indignation risked preventing the mantle of oblivion from covering all that. He came to agree. On our side, we banished the guilty party, a married man.'

According to some people, things weren't so clear. In that story, Strether had allowed himself to be duped despite his very real flair for picking out that type of black sheep.

There were insinuations, quickly dismissed, because Strether never lingered in the changing room, very modest, no unseemly stories about him. He was somewhat mannered, true, but he was a real gentleman, and you know the old saying: All gentlemen are actually ladies.

68

Max wanted to know more about the connections between the British Fascist League and the conservatives, a fringe group of conservatives who were pleased to mix with the blackshirts, who financed them a bit, but Strether was too discreet, so Max went to the big meeting in September 1930 in London, it promised to be historic, the places of honour were filled by members of very high society, gentry, financiers, newspaper magnates, a few lords, actors, all of them came to soak in the hardened enthusiasm of meetings, and some conservative sympathizers applauded as loudly as the members of the party, even shouted their disapproval when the dissenters, Jews and Communists, right? tried to speak. And applauded when the security force intervened, punches, clubbings, kicking, blood, cries, and obviously in these situations there are always two or three women who are dragged on the ground in front of reporters.

Max had seen all that, and the frowns on the faces of some of the conservative guests, the same ones who'd been applauding a few moments earlier. 'It was a bad image for what we wanted,' Strether said later, 'law and order. It wasn't my fault, the president had worked them up right before the meeting.'

That day Max had seen two newspaper owners tiptoeing to the exit. There were fewer articles sympathetic to the British Fascist League, fewer donations.

Max didn't tell Strether what had struck him the most, not the blows given by the security force, even if that time the dissenters had been somewhat older, no, what had seemed remarkable to him was a discreet gesture, not from a member of the security force, not a blackshirt, no, but from a man in a suit, very elegant, with a coat, pearl-grey scarf, a nice hat of the same colour, he seemed to have come from a board meeting or a social club, in short, Max saw him join the blackshirts while delicately slipping onto his right hand the four large metal rings that make up the 'brass knuckles'.

69

'It'll look really good in my piece,' Max said to Strether, 'the story of the meeting, the failures, it will give it an element of truth. Do you have any others like that? Someone told me about a story of a dairy, at Bethnal Green . . .'

Max's eyes widened, he had just caught Strether off-guard, shown him that he was doing his job in the field, that he had other informants.

'Oh,' said Strether, 'the dairy at Bethnal Green, a stupid incident, we were supervising a demonstration against a strike at a large dairy, a procession in front of the picketers sponsored by the Communists, we'd rushed the picketers, the police stupidly tried to intervene, I was even taken to the station, you know. But we didn't make that mistake twice.'

Strether hadn't given the order to desist in front of the police, he got angry at a sergeant, he accused him of working for the Reds and the Jews, he was taken to the station, he was threatened with a sentence for inciting a riot. And worse, he had an unregistered revolver on him, a service revolver. Strether didn't have a permit, it could have been very serious.

The inspector leading the inquiry was a veteran of the battles of Flanders in 1917, 1918. With tears in his eyes Strether told him that he knew the law but that he had never been able to separate himself from a weapon that had saved his life.

Strether stopped his story at that point, when the inspector, moved, decided not to press charges. No need to tell Max that the inspector was about to drop the charges but that he had called his superintendent on the phone. The superintendent had said to retain Strether. Shortly before 7 p.m., the quiet hour at police stations, the superintendent had appeared, accompanied by a man wearing a DSO, yes, he, too, and he had left the man alone with Strether. The man had said to Strether to call him Cox, Jeremy Cox, no more, he had spoken with a clear voice, not harsh, a voice that one must use in a centre of operations, an undynamic voice but one that doesn't hesitate, because hesitation gives death one more chance.

At the police station this Mr Cox had proceeded slowly, and each round of questions gave Strether the feeling that a trap was about to open beneath his feet and that it all depended on his interlocutor.

Cox had begun with a few details on matters relating to the security forces of the party, 'Yes, three of your men, injuries inflicted on a mounted officer, that's what happens when you throw a police officer off his mount, the file has been put aside, you will obviously be considered responsible, two broken bones, not too serious, when one has lived through what we have, it's almost nothing, but the younger generation has become oversensitive.' Strether had been a bit reassured by Cox's 'what we have lived through'.

Cox had also spoken of the affair of the young boxer, the rumours that had circulated, 'Useless to open an inquiry into what happens among your young men, right? Everyone trusts you,' Cox smiled, then abruptly changed the subject. 'You like London, it's pretty different from Birmingham, isn't it? There are difficult moments in life, but you've done very well for yourself, it's true that a man of your calibre is resourceful.'

Strether didn't really like him mentioning Birmingham, also, this Mr Cox had not insisted, he had merely asserted his own ideas, he had remained a bit of a soldier, if one might say so, yes, a high-level position in the defence department of the country and the Empire, 'My primary task is to be in the loop, I find your organization, your league, a bit excessive in what it proclaims, but in the long term we have approximately the same objectives, we believe that the principle threat is the Red menace, on almost the same scale today there is also the foreign menace, the foreign variant of the Red menace. You're not a threat, but I don't want to be caught off-guard, I must stay informed, obviously I am not going to demand that you tell me if you expect to travel abroad, wherever it might be, but we should keep a certain spirit of, let's say, chivalrous exchange between us.'

71

Strether and Jeremy Cox saw each other on several occasions after their first interview at the police station, and Cox had spoken again about travelling abroad and the chivalrous spirit, enough to allow a few figures from the court of King Arthur to pass between them.

Strether then wondered where Cox might have obtained those sorts of details. They weren't very specific, only shadows, he might of course know of Strether's travel plans from loud mouths in the party, and the allusion to the chivalrous spirit could be innocent, but even so.

'Anyway,' Cox had said, 'for those trips we can make things easier for you, papers, visas. I will just need the exact spelling of your name, William Gordon Strether, with an *h*, very good.

'What interests me is the foreign travel, what is being planned abroad, that's where we can really work together, not Birmingham, or London, I repeat, the main threat is the Red threat, but we must have a view of the whole picture, the Empire is threatened, in India, but there are secondary threats, right on our streets, yes, I'll take care of all the paperwork, seals, we can trust each other. My task isn't easy, Colonel, we are living under a Labour government, I must give them what they want, they want to know what is going on in Germany, in Italy, I have to be efficient. I sensed I could count on you.'

Strether found that Mr Cox had strange intuitions.

One day, as he was leaving, Cox had said to Strether, 'By the way, we have a friend in common, a French chap, Max Goffard, he's charming, but a bit long-winded, isn't he? And his American friend, does she ask a lot of questions?'

Strether hadn't liked what Cox was asking, he would have preferred to send him packing, but there was something he could no longer deny: Cox knew everything about Birmingham, had known it for a long time.

72

Strether had guessed right about Birmingham. Cox had spoken about it again, but only to tell him that it wasn't important, 'I know everything, dear Colonel, it is a fall that honours you, in Birmingham you did your job as a restaurant-owner very honestly, William's, it was William's, wasn't it? It was a very honourable establishment, good food, never any drunks, you closed at 10 p.m., one can't become rich with that format.'

And the end of William's had been unpleasant. In 1927, Strether had been forced into bankruptcy, a true dishonour, he couldn't bear it. He had decided to leave Birmingham as quickly as possible, to go back to London with his wife. There was something worse, and Cox must have known it—Strether had left Birmingham without going before the court that was to rule on his responsibility in the bankruptcy.

That was worse than being sentenced for bankruptcy. When you don't appear before the court, it is a serious offence that turns you into a fugitive, a suspect likely to be picked up by the police at any moment.

And in fact Strether should have been picked up for more than three years, the time it took for a court file to become a police file and to travel from Birmingham to London.

There were two possible explanations for this reprieve. The first, which Strether had for a long time believed, is that the court had many other fish to fry in London than a bankrupt restaurant-owner from Birmingham, especially at a time when there were thousands of bankruptcies every month, on every street of the country. The other explanation, which assumed more weight as the interviews between Strether and Cox continued, was that discreet hands had begun to put his file at the bottom of the pile each time the police should have taken an interest in him.

It was through his travels that Cox had succeeded in coming to an agreement with Strether. Strether needed to travel to gain importance in the party and Cox needed Strether's travel reports. He had facilitated his travels through customs and he had been rather satisfied with the results.

63

Max was beginning to get a little annoyed with Strether when he disappeared for four days. At the Regent, they told Max he was on holiday.

When he returned, Strether did not try to hide anything, 'I was in Germany, yes, it was my second trip, for the party. It was largely unofficial. I went to observe things, to soak up the atmosphere. Poverty, Max, that's what struck me, Germany is a country of orderly poverty. It's very hard in England, but Germany, it's hard to imagine how they are going to come out of it if they keep going like that, unless they make a great leap. It's very unusual. To go to Germany, excuse me for being obvious, one goes through France, where the trains are not on time, the porters cheat you, like the porters here, the toilets and the sidewalks are filthy, the people shout, fight, but the stores are full.

'When you arrive in Germany, the porters have a fixed fee, which they respect. The train schedule is also respected, there are a lot of conductors, but all the people are frighteningly thin. And in front of the stores, when a store is open, the people are in line, calm, a great army of famine.

'In the town of Kassel I saw people they call *sacks* because they carry a potato sack, an empty sack, they are on the dole but that's not enough to feed them, even less to feed their children, so they go on foot to the countryside, dig potatoes, that keeps them just on the edge of starvation. They have to fight against the farm dogs. Their backs have become bent from digging potatoes. The only time I saw them stand up was when the Brownshirts passed by singing. They didn't say anything, just stood up straight. Yes, I also saw some stand when the Reds passed by.'

74

'Yes,' Strether said to Max, 'in Berlin we were greeted by friendly groups. The Germans wanted to impress us.

It was annoying, sometimes. They looked down on us whereas we had beaten them soundly, in 1918. But in Berlin they showed us that they considered us a very small group. They said that England had not found its Hitler, that we were too influenced by the Italians and their Duce. They said that we should go beyond Fascism.'

Max could sense that the angels and the archers were about to return.

'We had a few conversations in a castle, far from Berlin . . .'

Strether lowered his voice but couldn't prevent himself from mentioning things that made him seem important.

'Max, it was as a veteran of Mons that I was finally respected in Germany, and because of the angels. The Germans did not believe in the angels, in any case not in ours, because they had another version, it was complicated . . . The idea of the recesses of history, with a hidden knighthood, King Arthur, the Teutonic knights, they were ready to make the connection, but they could not accept that we could have been helped in 1914, what interested them was not Mons but the present, the connection with a very distant past, ultimately, they sought to restore that knighthood, on the scale of a Great Europe, and this is where we have a role to play, don't look at me like that, Max, you don't understand, we don't have enough legend, we need Valkyries and heroes, we need to build a European legend, with apparitions, yes, we, too, why don't we have a right to those apparitions? You know that many people today believe in apparitions, it matters.'

Strether had also given his report to Cox who was content to take notes without reacting, he had not exposed his innermost thinking to Strether, he had kept it for his boss, for teatime, 'Those Germans are crazier and crazier, secret ceremonies! With torches! In a castle! They are shopkeepers, failed journalists, low-level functionaries, and they are playing in a mediaeval castle!'

Cox's boss had gone one step further, 'I know homes in Surrey or Scotland where they wouldn't even hire them as porters, and they think they've returned to the time of Teutonic knights!' The two men had laughed. They had concluded their conversation with the hope that 'those people' would make their big mistakes sooner rather than later.

PART VIII

A Woman in London

75

The roughly two years spent in the country with Mark had reconciled Gladys to London and she had adored the theatre where she was hired. She did housekeeping, made tea, ran errands, brought the mail, seated the audience, sometimes sold tickets, sometimes helped with scenery and lighting, sometimes ran lines during rehearsals, sometimes acted as maid and dresser, and people treated her well.

She felt somewhat spared in the midst of these people who spent their time lying to each other, for good and for ill, always exaggerating, people who used their bodies and their voices for the craziest of whims, or, worse, refused to act, and when the director was at the end of his rope, the actor or actress picked up as if nothing had happened, repeated a gesture ten times, simplified it, watched for the smile of the director, and then fell again into a sluggishness that sabotaged the entire effort of the troupe, then once again began to obey like a child as soon as the opening night arrived, which delighted the director, but it wouldn't last, the actor or actress changed everything on his or her own initiative on the opening night, in front of the audience.

And the director called them whores, hacks, then he was quiet before their success, or expected the play to fail completely and to kill his actors before being killed himself by the producer, and everyone gathered for the next performance because they were a troupe, and because at least they knew each other, which avoided uncontrollable surprises, that's what Edward, the director, said, why should he put a pervert out the door when in the theatre, the stage and wings, perversity is the norm? Perverse or not, she loved them all.

76

Gladys had learnt to pay attention, she sometimes acted as a confidant to the actors, she had to listen to them, they used her to regain strength, to expel their anxieties, to transfer them to her along with the dress to wash and the shopping list, so that she sometimes went home trembling with exhaustion.

But that wasn't the worst. The worst was when one of them complained to her about the acting techniques the director imposed on him or her, and it was so unimportant, it would have taken so little for the director to be aware of his error, sometimes that little thing was a modification of the role of a partner, and it was there that one had to put one's foot down.

The director liked Gladys very much, he sometimes asked her questions, to have a fresh point of view, he asked her questions because she didn't say anything, that was what she had to resist, not be transformed into a messenger, because actors are like that, they can put you in a precarious position, have you killed by a director, lead you to destroy the credit you've earned over months, they do that only to act in a different costume or dress, or so that the partner remains seated instead of being placed, and noticed, at the front of the stage, they would never dare ask that of the director, nor even ask you to go ask the director, but they know how to suffer in front of you to the point that because you are generous you want to help them out.

She never succumbed to the temptation. And she had the feeling she had thus earned the respect, the confidence of the actors. And one day, while she was fixing the hair of an actress who had become her friend, a voice had said through the door of the dressing room, 'Darling, it's Taylor, are you alone?' The actress had replied, 'Yes, come in!'

77

In spite of the 'are you alone?' incident, she couldn't help wanting to be there, at any moment, especially at the end of the performance, in the crowded dressing room, the men disappearing before the avalanche of women who rushed to see the actress. And, under the emotions of the evening, the stretching of nerves, there was hugging and kissing all round, in the midst of a mass of powder puffs, pots of cold cream, skirts, stockings, boxes with wigs. The actress was seated on a stool, her back turned to the harsh light of the shade-less bulbs that framed the large mirror, she received compliments about her talent, people told her that they would have liked at least ten more minutes, which could mean many things, and she repeated, 'Ah, my dears! My dears!'

Then the actress shot Gladys a friendly and somewhat pointed look. Gladys left the dressing room, without resentment, and went to help straighten up the stage, in the midst of the comings and goings of the machinists, the extras transformed into stagehands, all trying to prove themselves indispensable, and the scenery rose up from the floor, a lamp threw one more beam into the shadows, onto a fireman's helmet, onto a bit of scarlet fabric, all of that bathed in the smell of the theatre, rice powder, tobacco, gas, the smell of wood, mixed with the peppered dust of the wings, the smell of machine oil, the smell of paint and glue from the scenery, everything she could no longer live without.

One day, a director waiting for an actress who was late asked Gladys to play the wife to a man in uniform, it was a scene from a marriage, she knew the play by heart, he asked her to act meanly, she did so, then scornfully, with the will to destroy her husband, and she did, and while she was acting the director complimented her, she anticipated what the officer standing before her was going to do, it was easy, it was a character as predictable as Mark, as all men, and, as she anticipated, the officer seemed constantly to do what she predicted, she played the wife and at the same time, in her head, she anticipated the role of the man, as if he had been her puppet, and that female character was as hard and as mean as a man.

It was fantastic. And the actor who played the officer was increasingly unhappy, he kept looking at his watch, in the wings, into the seats, and he kept interrupting so she couldn't find a true rhythm, but she went back to the script, euphoric, she knew she didn't have the physique of a beautiful actress, that she would never be successful, but that morning she allowed herself to be carried away by her voice, her voice was capable of creating something on the stage.

Then the real actress arrived.

78

Gladys worked at the theatre for two years. She began early in the morning, and went to the back of the dressing rooms to the stockrooms. She tried on the costumes one after the other, entered into the characters, spoke to herself in front of the mirror, became Queen Elizabeth, Mary Stuart, a lady in waiting, she played Mary Stuart until her death and returned to announce the news to the Queen and became angry as the Queen, who hadn't wanted that death, that death had been stolen from her, it was difficult to play, because Elizabeth herself was an actress of superior talent, you couldn't show absolute anger—that death was very beneficial to her—or false anger because something had really escaped her control and made her furious.

And so she tried on all the characters. She almost managed to be Henry VIII but she found him too virile. She especially liked to become emotional while pretending to move her audience. She discovered she was capable of improvising.

She saw herself well in the role of the lover of a hero, she looked for the right one, her hero had been dead for a long time. She hadn't lost hope. That was also why she found Elizabeth difficult, she was a queen without a man.

In the evening, during performances, when she had a free moment, she loved to watch the play from the third balcony. There was a technical room that looked outside and from which one could also see the wings and the stage. She could see two actors performing a scene between a married woman and her lover, while the husband was waiting—joking in the wings with the theatre manager—to make a dramatic entrance. She saw the stage, she saw the audience, she saw the wings, slipped from one world to the other, delightfully, the only one able to do so.

She ended up becoming indispensable to many members of the troupe and began to have small roles, with lines.

79

One morning the troupe's producer took off and the troupe disbanded. Gladys had made friends, they didn't call her any more. She went to look at the water from a bridge over the Thames, the dark water offered oblivion. She returned home with heavy legs and an empty head. She didn't want to go back to the country. She reluctantly settled back into hunger and fear.

Every day she had to find something to eat, money for the rent. Above all, she couldn't spend her money on food. Money was for rent, because if you didn't have a room you were done for, a room with running water, cold water and a small basin, but running water, the only luxury, and not in just any neighbourhood, not in one of those neighbourhoods where the women dried their laundry in the middle of the street, not on just any street but on a street with lamps, she chose Bloomsbury, a room on the ground floor, damp, it smelt like a cellar, a bad building but with a good address. In the evening, coming home, she could see—through the windows of the houses—walls covered with books. When there weren't books, there were paintings.

She also had to have simple but always clean clothes, without trying to appear chic because when you're poor chic means you're ashamed, no, to appear as someone in whom one could have confidence in a dining room, before a clientele, whom one could send to people's homes. The best solution was to find work where one was fed, at least at noon. She knew she couldn't make a mistake, she didn't even have the resources of those women who, on Monday, brought their clothes to the pawnbroker for a few shillings because they knew that on Saturday they'd be able to buy them back with their husband's paycheques, you don't have a husband, you have only the evenings of a poor woman, and you need your clothes every day. There were a few simple rules to follow, one could get by.

She ended up developing a true talent for finding work, she knew whom she could ask 'Can I lend a hand?' with a real chance of being answered in the affirmative, you couldn't go into every restaurant and ask 'Might you have work?' it was useless, you became exhausted walking quickly, no, walk slowly, the time it takes to look through a window to see that an owner and his wife are unable to meet the demand, at the busiest of times, they'll lose customers, ask them the question at that moment, for a shilling, yes, right away, and work well, and since the rent was paid you could give a real address in the event they might need you again, a delivery woman at nine o'clock, a waitress at noon, rarely in the evening, the evening customers think they can get away with anything.

80

On several occasions she also worked in homes, as a replacement for a maid, she didn't like doing it, it was more regular work but without a break. Compared to pre-war times, things had changed a bit, the bosses avoided insulting, beating or shouting, but you also had to take care of the children and bring up coal, and answer 'Very well, ma'am' to the pleasant voice who asked you how you were, because if you answered that you were tired, they had qualms about making you work so hard and then it was the door. One of the most difficult experiences was a home in Scotland, with a Lady Wexford, a widow, a woman with a hard face who used creams and powders to battle against the necessity of ageing.

You're a maid and you wait in front of the chateau in the rain because you don't have an umbrella and you aren't allowed to get into the car before the mistress is settled, you have to wait to open the door for her and help her get in, and you sit in the front, with the chauffeur, like in the war, in ambulances.

The countryside is beautiful in Scotland, even when it rains, the rain washes the grass, the leaves, all the green, everything outside is beautiful when part of your life is spent in a room below ground in the chateau, the narrow roads, the rows of hedges, white fences, the grey-blue paths with silex sparkling at the slightest ray of the sun, horses in the meadows, who have learnt to no longer be afraid of cars and who start galloping along their fences to escort you for a moment, it lifts your spirits just watching them.

And it rains again, but the rain isn't enough to make you want to give up the countryside, sometimes you have to stop in spite of the rain because *her ladyship* has tapped on the separating window, you turn round, she doesn't want to shout, she simply holds up her thermos bottle, which means that as usual she can't manage to open it, she is riding in a car with a chauffeur and a maid and she is even more helpless than the worst alcoholic tramps, the chauffeur stops along the side of the road, you get out, you walk round the car, you open the door, you open the thermos bottle, it is pouring rain, your coat has been soaked for a long time, you serve the tea in the cap of the thermos bottle, you wait for the mistress to finish, she makes a face, it is her way of thanking you, you take back the cup, you empty it out, you put it back on, you put the thermos back, you get back into the car, you start off again, the only redeeming moment is when the chauffeur gives you a friendly smile, you are not alone.

81

You would have also forgiven *her ladyship*'s behaviour towards you when you finally arrive at the home of a cousin of *her ladyship*, when *her ladyship* is told as she gets out of the car 'You've aged a bit more,' you think it's just a joke, but the majestic cousin, his hand on the head of a huge Irish hound, a wolf hound, adds 'Be careful not to fall, or I'll send you to nursing care' in a voice that indicates that he will do just that, and that he has the power to do it, in short, during the long weekend *her ladyship* is treated like the lowliest pre-war chambermaid by her cousin, and in front of everyone, guests and servants, and *her ladyship* says nothing, 'He's so eccentric, isn't he?' 'Yes, Madame, very,' and what isn't said is that Madame depends on the cousin to buy even a slice of bread. The chauffeur puts it another way, he tells you that without the allowance the cousin pays her, *her ladyship* won't even have a pot to piss in.

And Madame is not the worst. At the cousin's chateau you learn a lot, in the evening in the kitchen, when you should go to bed and the servants exchange secrets to feel a bit less oppressed. 'You're lucky,' Carole tells you, 'mine is nice, but I haven't been paid in three months.' And she holds up one of her boss' blouses scornfully, 'Machine-made!'

Her ladyship's blouses are not machine-made, not the one you're washing at midnight because she decided before she went to bed that she wanted to wear it again tomorrow morning, and when *her ladyship* cries because of her cousin's meanness, you don't feel smug, because a woman treated like that will never have any human feeling, and you don't know how to leave her, because if you give notice she is capable of not giving you references, when a recommendation from *her ladyship* would make a difference, or she might say, 'You're not leaving, you're fired.'

The best is what actually happened—a new maid, recommended by *her ladyship*'s cousin, which made *her ladyship* sad to have to let you go and to replace you with a spy. She gives you references that describe you as having all the qualities that *her ladyship* expects not to find in the spy.

82

She sometimes also had pleasant surprises, like the day when, in another home, she realized that for some time she felt rather well, in a very stately home in Bayswater, with kind bosses, rich people who were honest, the staff had been there a long time, she had a room in the attic with a stove and a true sink with a bathroom at the end of the hallway, hot water, free time to read, one day off every week and two extra days to take during the month. There were lovely receptions, with polite people, a very correct majordomo who always took the trouble to tell the staff who was who at a soiree, a little restraint in his tone every time he uttered the name of a socialist or a singer.

One evening, she saw two maids with white aprons bordered with lace, large straps in a V, also bordered in lace, over black dresses with long sleeves, little white lace collars, small white caps that fell to their eyebrows, two maids side by side, their hands behind their backs, behind the end of a table set for a dinner for twenty people, three glasses, two plates, four sets of utensils for each person, five large bouquets of violets spread out along the table, a magnificent table runner of Indian embroidery, lovely red wine already in cut-glass carafes, and what you never saw at home, little bits of rainbows that sparkled in the cut glass of the crystal, the guests were about to arrive, one of the two maids seemed to be the leader, the tallest one, and the other had what indeed seemed to be the look of an oaf, dressed to the nines and awkward, as if terrorized by her partner, and the tall one was nothing but a mean guard dog, with the look of someone who felt it was her place to be there, in a lace collar, and all of that took place in a mirror, the tall maid was her.

At that moment she was repulsed at what she was becoming.

83

After leaving the Bayswater house Gladys returned to her life living day-to-day, she was never ill and managed to get along.

The afternoons were the most difficult, less chance of finding work or finding work that paid almost nothing, cleaning up, clean-up help. Only one interesting thing—delivering dresses after alterations. She went to a store-workshop that smelt like women, day-dreamed a bit while they were finishing with the package or listened to a department head complaining about seeing the British style fall victim to French and American influences, victim to the abandonment of soft curves and beautiful masses of fabric, in favour of 'outfits' that turned the chic London woman into a bare-legged pseudo tennis-player, 'Great couture is now made with the cut of scissors, my dear, rectangles, tubes, you see more and more skin, less and less fabric, soon we will send our dresses through the mail in envelopes.'

Gladys listened while calculating the tip she would be paid, because of the care that had been taken with the dress. It rarely met her expectations. There were also hats, which paid little, but the stylists were more human, they complained less about fashion, although hats were tending to have narrower brims, they were happy to talk to her, sometimes they even asked her a question about her own tastes.

84

Gladys could only do the afternoon errands on behalf of establishments where she was known, and the responsibility for the delivery was on her own head, that is, she had to sign a receipt that could send her in front of the judge at the least suspicion of theft.

She was afraid but she liked the rhythm, darting between cars, trucks, carts, the asphalt, the cobblestones, sometimes the dirt, the obstacles and the craziness of things, London was, in spite of the crash, in constant movement, she felt it stretching out further every day, she felt she was participating in the progress of the city, in the way it had of swallowing up huge pieces of countryside on its outskirts, or, in some neighbourhoods, on its last empty lots, which it gobbled up with scoops of a mechanical shovel, mouthfuls of stubborn dandelions and thistles that had nevertheless held up for centuries. And the city was also eviscerating itself, digging into the land to unheard-of depths, in huge worksites for pitiless buildings, it even dug under the water, made men work with compressed air tanks to build bridges, it also placed rails, allowed automobiles to go from twelve to twenty miles per hour, and buses went from fifteen to fifty passengers, and there were female police officers who managed the traffic, maybe she would become a female police officer, one of those she saw controlling with her raised hand the buses that raced round, competing with rival companies to get passengers, and on the Thames the firemen inaugurated their new fire boats that were twice as large, twice as powerful, and the city remained the largest in the world, bigger than New York, this was where one had to be, even if the newspapers told you that there were hundreds of thousands of people out of work, the city was full of crowds and Gladys walked in the city, from crowd to crowd, without belonging to any of them.

85

And the fear returned, in new ways every day, when, for example, Gladys ran into a man in the street pulling a horse cart himself, the rigging attached to his shoulders, and in one hand holding the lever that served to move the forward axle, and she couldn't bear it.

And when she had to go shopping at the market for an employer, she could never walk, without trembling, in front of the women who were shelling peas, especially since she had learnt that some of them had been doing it for more than fifty years.

In the evening, returning home, she repeated, 'I can read, I can write, I dress well, can speak with words of more than one syllable, I have driven ambulances, I ran the office of a field hospital, I've built airplanes, I've been the head of a team, the model for a large window, I've worked in the theatre'—and she interrupted herself in the midst of her soliloquy because for the third time a newspaper vendor put under her nose the headline of the *Evening Standard*, 'Secretary Assassinated in the Heart of the City,' a vendor with a cap who cried 'Secretary assassinated' in a beseeching voice, a child, no more than seven years old.

Sometimes, when things were going very badly, the simple fact of looking at a boat with lighted portholes passing by on the Thames became a diversion. Then she went home to her building whose courtyard echoed the slightest sounds of a voice, a toilet flushing, pots banging. She would sometimes go by the library, and return home, books under her arm, without hiding them, sometimes being called a stuck-up whore behind her back by the neighbour women who couldn't bear seeing someone appear to belong to a world other than the one they were forced to inhabit.

And the next morning she would return to her life with great slaps of cold water on her face and body.

86

The most important thing for Gladys during this difficult period was that she made a new friend. It was almost essential for survival, to be two, two to pay the rent, to stay warm, to check that the fire in the heater had been extinguished before going to bed, to be able to take turns to light it in the morning, to face up to the owner at the end of the week, to be two in good times, as well, to walk together, to act on a whim and decide to buy a blouse, a book or even to go to the cinema, with or without boys, two to walk faster returning home at night because you suddenly don't hear any voices in the street, no more doors shutting, no more cars, no more footsteps.

Her friend was named Marian, a fun-loving girl who had taught her how to avoid dancers with roving hands.

They would stroll jauntily, arm in arm, through London, or would wait for each other at the end of the day and go together to the pubs open to women, or to the least expensive music hall, for the warmth, the laughter, to feel a crowd that wanted to live. They couldn't get enough of that nocturnal London, of its lights above all, whose numbers were increasing daily, becoming stronger and stronger, transforming avenues into a single huge shop window. Lights that fought against the shadows without being able to rid the city of its halo of grey dampness.

Sometimes, too, they would stop upon the request of a woman or a man in uniform, agree to take a small printed paper and to sing on the sidewalk 'We shall sleep on that beautiful shore' with the accompaniment of the trumpets, saxophones and tubas of the Salvation Army.

87

This new friendship between Gladys and Marian had plunged them into a little euphoria that did not last.

The depression had made people increasingly violent, people were beginning to fight in lines, looking for jobs, they both began to feel increasingly threatened.

On winter evenings, when they returned in the fog and raised their heads to the light of a street lamp, they had the feeling of being pulled along by a slow stream of yellowish water, glittering with frost, that flowed above them, between the walls of the buildings, and that would ultimately submerge them.

A neighbour woman coped better. Everyone knew how she did it, since she would sometimes be brought home in a car by a customer. She didn't hide it, said it was 'temporary'.

Marian and Gladys had begun by joking a bit about it while eating their bread and soup in the evening. Then they talked about it more often. They discussed, hesitated, had a pet term for it, joked of 'doing a bit of temporary'. And finally the decision—anything but that, because even if one survives it, you never get over it.

They left London for Birmingham. Marian knew the city, they would have more chances of surviving there than in London. They would be able to find better work, a new life, maybe even a man for each of them,

'You know, in Birmingham we'll have the cachet of being women from London,' said Marian, 'we are quickly going to meet some interesting men.'

PART IX

A Man in Birmingham

88

One day, at Max's pleading, Strether agreed to talk about Birmingham. He had stayed for some time in the city, 'Yes, that's where I met my wife.'

No, in Birmingham he wasn't a maître d', he'd been a restaurant-owner.

And Max imagined a Strether who was even more imperious than in London, but in a smaller world, enough to whet the appetite to move up to the capital. He could imagine the scenario—a restaurant-owner with class, word got out, he wanted to go to London, a veteran, the Regent needed a maître d' . . .

'Did you have a speciality? Any specific dishes?'

'Nothing fancy, it was a restaurant to fill stomachs, hearty soups, meat, stews, sausages, potatoes, I became a specialist in Cumberland sausages, at least they looked good on the plate, they're different from Frankfurters, aren't they? Yes, I also got married in Birmingham, but quietly, as they say.'

Max wasn't able to learn more about the circumstances of how he met his wife. Strether was like that on the subject—he didn't avoid the question, he responded briefly, then the curtain fell. And Max could not allow himself to ask indiscreet questions of a married soldier, even one who, in the depression, has fallen to the rank of a waiter. Anyway, Strether performed his job with such elegance that Max chided himself for thinking of a word as common as 'waiter'.

Strether also used these story sessions with Max as a rehearsal, for the day when Cox would ask him for details about certain things.

89

Strether's restaurant had been rather successful, he described it with the love of a job well done, it had gradually become the meeting place for merchants, workers, veterans, with their families, their children, with ears that stuck out, who were scolded by their mothers from a glance by their fathers when they drew parallel roads with a fork in their mashed potatoes, a clientele that held certain principles and Strether would quickly, even before the client had made any remark, take a questionable glass or knife back into the kitchen in front of everyone. People smiled when he went by, holding the offending object, they called that 'the eye of the owner'.

'Yes, I liked that, the quality of the details, my restaurant was modest but I wanted people to feel that everything they were offered was done correctly. And I have an almost feminine sense of order.'

Like all restaurateurs, Strether earned more money with two glasses of liquor at the end of a meal than with the meal itself, but he didn't push customers to consume, he didn't like seeing his customers drinking too much, he wished to maintain a certain decorum, 'The false decorum of the middle class,' said the detractors of his establishment, in other words, his competition. But that didn't prevent the ambience of the restaurant from being rather joyful, with customers who went there to spend a moment that was different from those they experienced at work, on the street, at home.

90

'I thought I was going to be able to stay in Birmingham,' Strether told Max, 'and up to a point the restaurant wasn't losing money. It was hard but I liked it, it was very different from the Regent, of course, but I felt as if I was living in the true country. I talked with people who didn't look down on me.

'I watched the accounts, I managed, I lowered some prices, but what I couldn't predict was how the depression affected morale, how the people stop going to restaurants or bars, not because they don't have the money, you can always manage somehow, but because they no longer had a taste for anything. People liked each other less and less.

'And that terrible depression grew worse just when I was rediscovering a taste for the future. It took plutocrats, their madness, the lust for lucre, the golden calf, I hated them, they escaped beyond the borders, they disappeared. And it was people like me who suffered. Whereas there should have been discipline and organization.'

Strether's voice was calm and soft. Max respected his silences, didn't try to push him. He let Strether create his speech, let him enjoy that creation.

'I had to stop. There might have been a solution but I didn't want to try. My licence gave me the right to be open at night but I didn't like the night-time clientele in the country, wild-eyed drunks, people who vomit.'

91

'I learnt a lot in my Birmingham restaurant,' said Strether, 'an out-of-work veteran, for example, that's very tricky, much trickier to serve him than a rich man, if you pay too much attention he takes that as charity, not enough and he leaves, you can't be too human, he's come to your place to be treated as a customer, you have to act very quickly because the room is full and there's only three of you to serve some thirty tables, with a smile, and above all, while anticipating, you have to identify the customers who are going to take their time because their table has launched into an enthralling conversation, it is a table that can wait, but not another, the one where a man is scowling at his wife, you'll have to bring the cheque to him before all the rest, the best is to be there before he asks, he is surprised, he will return, maybe with someone else.'

Strether paused. His jaw clenched a bit, he looked straight at Max. 'By the way, someone mentioned you, not long ago, a Jeremy Cox. I learnt that he is *Sir* Jeremy Cox. We have common acquaintances that do us honour, don't we?'

Max smiled, he expected to hear more about Sir Jeremy but nothing came.

Strether continued to talk about his restaurant, Max took notes.

92

'There is also the noise of conversations in the dining room, Max, and that is like an orchestra—when people aren't making enough noise, your room is quickly lugubrious, when they make too much, the voices, the silverware, the laughter, the chairs, it becomes unpleasant, especially for the women, and make no mistake, it's the women who choose the restaurant, a husband wants to make his wife happy by taking her to the restaurant, and when there is a group, it's the same, the women have to be comfortable, it's a very simple detail but the women's toilets were impeccable, I said that the women should have the impression that they were spending the best moment of their week with me, even if it was in the company of their children, so I had to be careful of the noise, I had become an expert, when a table was too noisy I lingered a bit next to it, I made sure not to speak as loudly as they and they lowered their voices to hear me, when I left them they kept the same tone, at least for a few minutes. I really liked doing that.

'And there is that wonderful moment, when the room is full, when everyone has been served, when all is going well, a harmony, it doesn't last long, but I always looked out for that moment, it made me think of the theatre, the climax, then things start to go back to normal again, more disorder, tables are emptied, things calm down, it's not as busy, but not as pleasant, either.'

93

'And what I learnt in Birmingham served me well later, Max. For example, when I started at the Regent, I immediately identified the waiters who were working and those who held back, those who were careful not to tire themselves and pretended not to understand my look, I quickly had an excellent team, it's a matter of rhythm, like in rugby, when it works you're carried by the rhythm of the others, and I, from atop my few steps, I orchestrate, I know how to do it because, ever since Birmingham, I have the rhythm of my waiters in my legs, and if you go down into the dining room at the right time to help a young waiter who's overwhelmed, even if such a thing isn't done, you'll earn unlimited devotion, I go down when I see one of my waiters at the point that I, myself, would have liked for someone to help me in Birmingham, when I had no one, I go down, even if it's only to pick up a couple of dirty plates.

'You can't intervene too often, you have to maintain a balance, because if the customers see you with dirty plates too often, they won't speak to you in the same way any more, you have to do just what is necessary for them to say that you are a man who isn't afraid to get his hands dirty, but no more, but on the other hand a boss must sometimes act exactly on the same level as his men, it is important for the confidence they have in him, thus one or two dirty plates from time to time, it's part of the order.

'In the newspaper business you certainly have to carry dirty plates from time to time, or am I wrong, Max?'

94

'What was hardest to endure in Birmingham was obviously the end,' said Strether, 'but before that there was the strike of 1926, the demonstrators prevented buses and trams from moving, they sang, they raised their fists, there were days when one felt that everything could change, like in Moscow . . . Fortunately, there were volunteers who replaced the Reds . . . In any event, it was very difficult for business, they wanted to block deliveries, and when there weren't enough of them they insulted us. But there was the act that made it unlawful to provoke an apprehension of being exposed to hatred, ridicule or scorn in someone, the Reds could no longer insult the volunteers who took their jobs, some were fined ten pounds for a shout, they understood.

'That general strike to support miners lasted scarcely a week, it was a failure. And the strikers agreed to what they should have agreed to at the start, the low-ering of salaries, that's what is necessary during a depression. But people don't want to accept that.

'Yes, that's how I began to be interested in politics, because I wasn't getting any more meat or beer, and I was a veteran. I went to demonstrate against the Reds, with other veterans, and not just demonstrate, I agreed to perform certain tasks, filling in, along with students, I even drove a delivery truck to go back and forth between restaurants and fishermen and farms, I had someone with me, a young man from Cambridge, they aren't all Reds down there, his family had come across the Channel with William the Conqueror, we got along very well, together we reconstructed a society without weakness, we were that society, I really enjoyed those times, it reminded me of the war.'

95

'I had to close my restaurant. Abandon it entirely, Max. Wait, I'm counting on you here. I'm telling you everything, so you'll understand. But don't mention the bankruptcy, that stays between us, I kept my accounts well, but there's always a moment when you have to plan, it's almost a duty, I had the choice between stopping or planning, I tried to make it work for another year but things began to change from week to week, Max, do you really want me to relive all that?'

Max didn't ask for anything, he knew that Strether followed his own rhythm, that the colonel never stayed on this subject very long, that he always returned to London, to the party.

'I had told my president about some of my experiences in Birmingham, Max, without mentioning the bankruptcy, he's the one who told me about the job at the Regent, the party had treasury problems, I didn't cost them a lot but they thought it better for me to have a job outside the organization. The president told me that it would pose fewer problems with the other bosses, it would give more weight to my words, great debates were anticipated, my positions in favour of the current leaders should not appear to be dictated by my position as an employee of the party.

'The manager of the Regent is a sympathizer, things happened fairly quickly, they advanced me what I needed to buy two suits, yes, it is the sign of the quality of an establishment, you must be able to have your clothes washed quite often.

'I first worked alongside the current maître d', he was to be assistant manager at an establishment opening in Southampton, he was very good, I stayed behind him, I observed, and he left telling the young people in the dining room that I was a veteran of Mons, protected by the angels.'

96

During his other conversations with Strether, Jeremy Cox, Sir Jeremy, had asked him nothing about Birmingham. And as for his trips, the Germans had interested him a bit, then he didn't mention them again, he went on to other things.

It was bizarre. Strether expected him to try to extract information but it was Cox who talked, who spoke to him about a young politician, a hope of the Labour Party who had just quit the government and the party, a few months earlier.

'Yes, it was after that,' said Cox, 'that young Oswald Mosley began to interest me. Why? Because I find that, for a former Socialist, he utters the word *national* too often. Obviously, when one stays in organizations that lean too much on tradition it's not important, but when one has a lot of ambition, when one has broken with conservatives and Labour, when one has inherited the title of Lord and one has been successful in meetings, all of that turns you into a person to be watched, doesn't it?

'An old friend advised me to keep an eye on young Mosley, you must know him, a former First Lord of the Admiralty, who no longer has much of a future, I admit, but he's very clear on political matters, yes, Churchill.'

Strether had already served Churchill at the Regent. He was invited most often by a great newspaper magnate, Lord Rotherbrook. Strether suspected Lord Rotherbrook was picking up some of his friend's expenses. He said nothing to Cox.

Cox continued, 'It was Churchill who warned me—Mosley is seeking to create a new party. A new party at this moment in Europe is disturbing, especially when it threatens to have at its head a troublemaker who proclaims that "politics is a legitimate defence." It is the argument of those who are ready to do anything.'

97

Strether finally understood the deal Cox wanted to make with him—they wouldn't mention Birmingham again, ever, and Strether would infiltrate the 'new party' that Sir Oswald was organizing.

Strether didn't like Mosley, the man had squandered the credit he'd accumulated by waging a good war, the man who'd ruined women, the man who'd invented the slogan 'Vote Labour, Sleep Conservative'.

The debate took place in the ranks of the British Fascist League. Mosley was seductive. But Strether was unshakeable—one could not reconstruct greatness without the family, and the British family risked being destroyed if they claimed confidence in a man who exuded sexuality as soon as he crossed the threshold of a house where there was a woman who wasn't his. For Strether, marital infidelity was an infamy.

The militants found Strether rather old-fashioned, but the speech sat well with the sympathizers with whom he got together at the pub after meetings, with women, above all, of which there were more and more, they accompanied the men, they spoke little, but their facial expressions approved when Strether talked like that. The president of the party and the management team joked about it, but henceforth the women would be voting. In public, the leaders had the same position as the head of their security forces. They didn't want Mosley to take control. And Strether thought he was strong enough to turn down Cox's deal.

PART X

A Man, A Woman

98

The scene takes place in the Regent hotel. Two men in suits and overcoats enter the restaurant, or, rather, they change direction and head towards the lobby. The younger one stays behind while the older and better dressed one speaks to the head receptionist and asks for the manager. The receptionist has seen the man come in, recognized him, a police inspector. He suggests that the policeman first speak to the maître d', that's the hierarchical path. 'No, I want the manager, immediately, in person, that should be possible, shouldn't it?' The policeman adds something else under his breath.

There must be a panic button because the manager arrives in less than a minute, something very rare, it only happens when very important people come in unexpectedly, monarchs, heads of government, or, lately, a very great actress. The manager is a thin man with a face that never smiles, he doesn't greet the policeman but listens to him and then heads with him towards the dining room.

The dining room is Strether's domain, the manager must have something important to say to his maître d'. Strether hurries to him. The manager says something in his ear, Strether gestures to the second maître d', a sign that means, 'I'm putting out a fire, I'll be back, do your best,' and then, in his tailcoat, shirt front and hard collar, goes with the manager to the lobby.

The two gentlemen in overcoats say a few words to Strether and leave with him. As they pass, a porter rushes up, smiling, to hand Strether his hat and scarf. He takes only the scarf.

On the sidewalk two other men, this time in uniform, flank Strether and have him get into a vehicle. It all takes no more than two minutes. 'Strether taken off by the police, thrown into a paddy wagon,' cried Max, 'in less time than it takes to order lobster.'

'Please tell my wife,' was all Strether had time to say to the manager.

99

Strether went into the police station, the agents on duty stood up. They later said that they thought it was an inspection, a well-dressed big shot who had come for an inspection before going out on the town, it happens. All the same, Strether, it was noted later, was dressed as a waiter. If the agents on duty in London are no longer capable of distinguishing a waiter from a Scotland Yard boss, what's the world coming to?

The policemen who had stood up said that it was his general bearing and his way of raising his chin that gave Strether the impression of looking down on you, like someone who had something to settle with you, all the policemen were bothered, in any case, and not only those who stood up, the law is nevertheless clear, a bankrupt who has not appeared at his court hearing must necessarily be put behind bars. While waiting for a ruling on his fate, he is seen as being in flight, that's the law regarding bankrupts and Strether knew it.

It was also said, much later, that Strether was not expecting to be taken away, that he was counting on protection from high places, but that that protection did not happen, yes, it is known that Strether had attempted to invoke it that day, he had given a phone number to the inspector, and it was in fact that phone call that seems to have poisoned things, whereas the inspector had seemed very impressed by the details that Strether had given him, the receptionist claimed much later to have heard an expression such as Special Branch, even M15, but no one knew very much, especially not those who claimed that a certain Sir Jeremy was mixed up in all this, that it was he who had told the inspector to apply the law to the letter and so on, or that Sir Jeremy considered Strether to be a pariah, or that he was aware and was using the procedure to obtain something from Strether that Strether was refusing him.

A very upset woman also appeared at the police station, a Mrs Strether. The official had received the order to turn her away. He didn't even write down her name.

He did however tell her that her husband was going to be sent to the Brixton prison.

100

Strether left the police station in a little van, between a purse-snatcher and a man who had beat his wife too indiscreetly.

A woman was gesturing, on the sidewalk in front of the prison entrance, as the van drove in. Strether didn't see her.

The other accused moved aside to let him get out, and the guards stood at attention when he began to cross the courtyard. Having arrived at the intake, he carried out all the formalities with a great deal of dignity, he added 'Reserve Colonel, DSO' next to his name, he signed, then passed into another room, and that's where things began to deteriorate, when he refused to put on a prisoner's uniform, 'I am the recipient of the DSO, I shouldn't be undressed like a criminal, I will keep my own clothes on.' At first the guards tried to reason with him, they took their time with the gentleman, they gave an annotated reading of the regulations, it wasn't a humiliation, it was in his interest, his rights, Strether listened to the explanations, a guard added that the Colonel should understand that it was like in the army, 'And in the army one obeys, right?' the guards weren't there to humiliate him, they were representatives of a law that was being applied through regulations. He answered that he understood perfectly, but that he was going to be freed very shortly, at any minute, that he should not be subjected to a treatment that degraded him.

101

The others were beginning to get impatient, other prisoners were beginning to get undressed, they were cold, ill-humoured, Strether wouldn't give in, the veteran, the officer, the gentleman, the maître d' at one of the greatest restaurants in the world, was going to be ridiculed, his name destroyed, his reputation, for an error, false testimony, no doubt, they just had to wait, and it was out of the question that his picture be taken, either, he refused everything, the guards weren't fazed, they see this type of recalcitrant behaviour every day, all sorts of silliness, the prisoners try to stand out as soon as they arrive, especially the gentlemen, but, after verification, Strether was out of luck, he benefited from no particular recommendation and so five of them surrounded him, three with truncheons.

And just as the leader was putting his hand on Strether's shoulder, Strether shrank to the wall, sat on the ground, in a corner, his knees to his chin, his hands on his face, yes, unexpected, wasn't it? this man who had seen so much, the English have a word for this, he was *cornered*, he began to mutter, in a tearful voice, the voice of someone who has lost everything, 'Don't touch me . . . I'm a woman!'

PART XI

Much More a Woman

102

Things then happened very quickly for Strether—
Walthers, Gladys Walthers, was her real name.

The guards turned her over to a prison doctor from
Brixton who indelicately confirmed the total absence of
'external genitalia' and the presence of 'small but present
breasts'. They immediately transferred this Mrs
Walthers to the woman's prison in Holloway.

For his part, the inspector had insisted on going in
person to the Regent to inform the manager. He wasn't
obligated to do so but he found the errand to be rather
pleasurable. For once, the manager wouldn't assume
great airs. To have a maître d' who was a bit of a thief,
that can happen to the most scrupulous of managers,
can't it? But not to notice for several years that one has
employed a woman instead of a man, that takes special
talent, one must not have a very firm idea of the difference between the sexes, and indeed, that now seemed
to be true of that falsely virile manager.

The inspector did not make that rather crude
remark, about the famous absence of a firm idea as to
the difference between the sexes, to the manager's face.
He simply suggested that there was perhaps a problem

but in a way that the manager perhaps found more insulting than a reproach. Because when one is manager one can accept that a more socially frustrated man, a neighbourhood inspector, will show obvious surprise when he is faced with certain facts, one can pardon him an expression such as 'But really, how is it that no one noticed anything?' one can then explain to him the true complexity of the large world that is the Regent. But a man who, with the pseudo-accent of an honourable college, stresses that the police identification procedures have very quickly enabled them to unmask a sexual impostor, that man is suggesting that your procedures, the manager of one of the greatest places in the world, are useless.

The manager hadn't reacted, just allowed himself a smile that was all the more amiable since he was thinking that the inspector was a dirty bastard.

103

The inspector then went to the home of Gladys Walthers aka Colonel Strether. He found his so-called wife there, a tall woman with grey eyes, rather pretty, but sad. She already knew everything, no doubt thanks to the Regent's manager.

She protested. She really was married to the colonel, yes, a wedding in Birmingham. Her name was Marian, nee Liddell, a housewife. She claimed she knew nothing about the deception. For her, the colonel was a man. And, if she understood the inspector's question, she had never had what the inspector called 'natural relations' with the colonel, they didn't get married for that sort of thing but to be together in life.

The inspector suspected a different story but it was going to be very difficult to establish the facts. First, he had to verify when and how the marriage had been recorded.

The house was well kept.

104

Max was quickly informed of what had happened. Sir Jeremy told him late in the morning the next day, in Hyde Park, during a conversation that he had previously told Max was *necessary and urgent*. 'We might have done something stupid,' he said to Max, 'not we ourselves but we missed an opportunity to prevent something stupid from being done.'

Max was dumbfounded, Strether was a woman, or, rather, a woman was posing as Strether, a married woman, 'Yes,' Jeremy Cox had continued, 'our Gladys really is married to a certain Marian Liddell, it seems you met her, a rather pretty girl with grey eyes.' Max couldn't hide his anger.

Later, in Paris, he would confide in some friends—those English bureaucratic peasants didn't even know the heart of the story, they only knew about the bank-ruptcy in Birmingham and the usurpation of the military rank, that's all, nothing else! Cox even confessed that if he had known, he would have pushed the game further. He acted without delay and without heart, that'll teach him, when one has a profession like his one doesn't seek revenge.

Sir Jeremy waited, smiling, for Max's anger to dissipate, he helped him calm down by asking him how many times he had spent an evening with the 'colonel' without experiencing the slightest doubt. 'I would like you to continue to see this person,' he then said, 'I can't get mixed up in it, not me or my services, we won't be able to prevent the scandal, *the colonel was a woman*, it's a headline that's worth too much money for everyone, we aren't going to be able to keep the press away for more than two days, and I have no interest in speaking to them about national security, there's going to be a huge scandal, and we'd like to see to it, in light of our previous discussions with him, with her, we would like things to go as smoothly as possible, if I may say so.'

105

Max and Sir Jeremy finally sat down, 'No, Max, not the lounge chair, the bench, I prefer the bench, it's more comfortable, we don't want this person to feel too resentful, you might tell her that I didn't know anything about her true identity, it's true, I thought that a little reminder of her past bankruptcy wouldn't hurt, but, if I had known the rest, I wouldn't have committed that stupidity, what she accomplished is admirable. Do you realize what we could have done with her? You know I helped her to travel to Germany? She came back with stories of knights, an order of knights that those idiots in brown shirts were trying to reconstruct, we had a good laugh.'

Max had his own idea about the laugh that Strether had shared with Sir Jeremy, but he didn't try to disabuse his interlocutor.

106

Sir Jeremy had assumed a very friendly tone. 'Max, I'm asking you this as a personal favour, of course, all sorts of things are bound to happen, the exclusive interview, the story of her life, perhaps a contract for her memoirs, tell her that we're not opposed to anything, she'll have the right to tell everything, but without exaggeration, right? No novels, we're not in a Mrs Christie novel. A personal favour Max, you can't say that I've ever let you down.

'Have you noticed? It's impressive today, these enormous grey masses, the agitation of the clouds, it's changed the past few days, the sky without warning, I'm becoming a poet, but we owe, . . . oh, those pigeons!'

At their feet three pigeons were pecking increasingly violently at the gravel on the path, and one of them, as if inadvertently, had just attacked Sir Jeremy's shoes.

'It's like with people, Max, these pigeons are too coddled, they're becoming aggressive.'

Max didn't answer, he'd had this discussion with Sir Jeremy who was one of the reactionary undesirables that Max, for a lot of reasons, was forced to frequent.

'Where was I? Right, we need to end this story. We're going to facilitate things so that you can have access to Strether-Walthers. She must be beside herself, you must reassure her quickly, tell her if things go well there will most likely be no prison time. You see what I'm getting at, Max, I'm speaking in adverbs, I don't like it, in addition your French adverbs are rather long.'

107

Max was very attentive to what Sir Jeremy was saying. He sensed he was anxious, there were going to be things to negotiate.

There was, however, a moment when Max was distracted, when he thought of the face Lena was going to make, not easy to follow the speech of an officer in the M15 when one is thinking about what one is going to say to a beautiful woman, *you know, your handsome warrior* . . . he began to hesitate about how he was going to tell Lena, *yes, the colonel, in reality he is a tranie, no, not what you think*, he would have to let Lena arrive at the truth, *no, it's even better, he's a real woman* . . . there would be a moment of humour, the only difficulty was the expression *tranie*, dangerous, such words with Lena, to be avoided, say rather, *a true female, your colonel's a false colonel and a true female*, it was less shocking but less dangerous, how could he get to Lena before the newspapers did?

'The newspapers will go wild,' said Sir Jeremy, 'they're going to descend on the prison, I've men posted at Strether's home, and there is the question of his *wife*, she is very accommodating, at least, this will give us one less Fascist party, with the stories that are going to get out, this Fascist League is going to have trouble arranging meetings. That said, it doesn't resolve anything, the militants will go to other parties, I don't like those people, they're always on the verge of illegality, it's ok for Italy or Germany but Great Britain was not born in the last century, after all, Max, we have rules.'

They stood up, walked along the banks of the Serpentine.

'All the same, I would have liked to work out one little thing with Strether, yes, an intuition, a little intuition, I'll have to tell you about it, it's about this Mosley, we're not hiding anything from each other, right? I don't like him very much, he's beginning to mix national and socialist and he's having some success.'

Sir Jeremy seemed softened. He took Max by the arm. He didn't recall the war, the time when they worked together, behind the German lines. He simply said, 'It's been a while since we exchanged favours.'

108

The same day, late in the afternoon, Max was able to pay a visit to Gladys. She was wearing shapeless clothes under a sort of smock, she smiled when she saw Max, quickly understood.

She did not prove difficult, she would never speak to anyone about her little discussions with a certain high-level bureaucrat, she mainly wanted to explain herself to Max.

'We'd become friends, I have failed our friendship, Max.'

'And even good manners, Madame.'

'We had to survive, Max, you understand, survive above all, I couldn't go back to the country, and London for a woman alone, without anything, you know what that can be, while in Birmingham, a man, a woman, it didn't take more than a few hours to find a small apartment. And a few more days to find the restaurant.

'And then it became intoxicating, Max, to be able to talk about politics, history, war, everything, at a table full of attentive, respectful men . . . you don't need to shout, on the contrary, you're a man, you lower your voice, and without speeding up you choose your words, the men wait, without looking at you like you're some sort of anomaly, you've become the best among them, you don't believe it, of course, but they make you feel it, you have ideas and it's not strange, you can speak like a man, with the statements of a man, weighty statements with background, heavy with manly experience, all the statements I'd previously found pretentious, I learnt to use them, to like them. When a woman says "Effort leads to success," you believe her, it's a formula that works well in the kitchen, or with children, but to say something a bit more paradoxical, while smiling, something like "Success incites effort, and habit facilitates success," you have to be a man, if a woman says that you immediately think that she has read it or she is quoting her husband or someone else, it doesn't have the same resonance as when a man says it, men and women cannot attribute a statement like that to someone who makes jam, those statements were often pretentious but for me they were intoxicating, Max.'

109

'And I gave them cane-fighting lessons, Max, they watched me, I almost didn't have to do anything, a few gestures, corrections, Mark taught me cane-fighting so I could defend myself on any occasion with an umbrella,

I wasn't a very good teacher, they wanted to do well, and they improved. I also gave them lessons on women, I loved that, to warn them about gold-diggers, I loved listening to the men talk about women, that mix of vulgarity and naivety, so easy to manipulate, I didn't think men were so stupid on that level, they think they're very savvy because they say *cunt* or *pussy* but that's their weakness, it's enthralling, and they asked me for advice, I gave them warnings, I advised them to keep their distance, hoping it would prevent any problems, for the women, I mean, my dear sisters, always ready to be taken in, to be coquettish before compliments, anyway, I don't like coquettish women.'

'When she said *coquettes* she meant *pretty women*,' Lena commented when Max told her about his conversations with Strether in the prison meeting room.

110

'The most pleasant thing,' Gladys said, 'was that as Strether I no longer needed to have confrontations. When you're a woman and you want to get out of what is imposed on you, you always have to confront, step up and face it. You're at the table—if you want to say something in the middle of a talk among men, you have to interrupt, be annoying, no one says anything to you, no man is going to interrupt, especially if the table is filled with gentlemen, they simply glance at each other.

'Do you know what I mean, Max? to talk while the others are looking at each other? Even women play that game, exchange glances with the men who are listening to you, as if asking them to pardon their gender for including such an outrageous representative as this one, one who has dared to insinuate herself into a conversation on Indian politics or the lowering of salaries, what is worse is that they dream of doing the same thing, of speaking up to say important things, but when they see another doing it they are mostly sick at the idea that another is threatening to become freer than they, and they readily belittle the women who try to be too forward with their looks. Since I became a man, I could enter into that world of looks without betraying anyone. I could even look down on the suffragettes, not down on them, I never looked down on them, but from a distance, it was wonderful to be able to say: "Women shouldn't step too far out of their role."'

111

'In fact, Strether was very educated,' Max told Lena. 'Her parents allowed her to become a teacher, she read a lot, history books and novels, she's an expert on Henry VIII and Elizabeth I but she didn't go to teacher school. She was the energetic and simple girl who fled to London when her reading gave her the desire for something other than a room full of children and tea with the pastor's wife. Her eyes were opened before the picture postcards, Harrod's windows and the Piccadilly posters, she got drunk on the air of the Thames. She hadn't yet seen what went on in the back streets, she didn't need to go there, she didn't yet have to live there.

'In the end, the war was her ticket out. She didn't have time to settle down when she was young. She gradually ate up her nest egg, she encountered her lieutenant, she became a war widow, an ambulance driver, a worker. She experienced poverty and dealt with it, she didn't have work but she had experience, appetites. Her second marriage with a fool enabled her to be done with false solutions. Not to mention that this second husband and his mates gave her the experience of being round rather awful men. She stored away her repugnance and became ready for her disguise.'

112

The opportunity presented itself during the train ride to Birmingham. Gladys had dressed as a man for the trip, very chic, a dark grey suit she'd taken when the theatre troupe disbanded. She did that to be able to smoke in the train without being looked at askance. On several occasions men addressed her as 'sir' and she immediately played the part. Marian couldn't believe it. Before they left, Gladys had told her that, at the theatre, she'd sometimes taken the masculine roles during rehearsals, had sometimes played small roles in performances, a presence, a valet, a father-in-law, no more that that but it had always worked well.

And in their compartment they overheard the conversation of some working men, young fellows who spoke loudly about women taking the work of men, that's why there was the depression, the pastor had said so, women who don't want to stay home any more, you agreed to give them the right to vote and now you see the result, the pastor had said.

One of the three young men had said to Gladys, 'If you please, sir, what would you say if your wife wanted to work outside the home?' Placing her hand on Marian's arm Gladys had calmly replied that he would find that disagreeable, that he had not been wounded in the battle of Mons to see such a thing happen.

113

Marian was expecting a catastrophe at any moment. But Gladys boldly continued, in a slow voice, choosing her words to talk about weighty things, and the three working men nodded their heads, they were less well dressed than Gladys, they were trying to identify the elegant man speaking to them, who had spent four years in the war, when they, 'Yes, we were too young to go.' They found this man in a dark suit a bit affected, stiff, like someone who has money problems but who doesn't want to show it, he agreed with them, he said what they themselves thought, better than they could have done, a man who weighed his words and knew how to use them, he probably had financial difficulties but he held on to his status as gentleman, his gestures betrayed his rank.

Strether immediately assumed a slow voice, said Max, sometimes that delayed him in the conversation but it was necessary because he had to be careful with his words, to get rid of anything feminine. For her gentleman's demeanour, she was careful, she was always very discreet about her origins and took care so that the smartest of her interlocutors would think of a ruined old family or of a ruined member of an old family, members of the nobility never have a very virile look, do they, but they can die when necessary, walk into fire their heads held high, under their feminine demeanour.

114

They settled in Birmingham, Gladys permanently as a man. Marian immediately noted the change. She was respected because she had become the wife of William Strether, reserve colonel, DSO. Marian was a smart girl. She had to change her style. She could have done it with humour but it was difficult. Gladys had taken over the management of the restaurant, with her suit and her medals she had no problem, she found unemployed

men to work in the kitchen and wait tables, she supervised, took orders, managed the till, served customers
who seemed important, with enormous energy, she was
ecstatic.

At the beginning Marian did a little cooking, then
the till, but the men had a tendency to joke round with
her and Gladys said that that would one day cause problems, a reserve colonel could not permit men saying certain things in front of his wife, it would be better if
Marian took care of their home, it would be easier. Marian had to turn herself into a good housewife.

There were probably conflicts at that time, said
Max, but Strether never said much about it. That said,
it's not difficult to imagine. Marian didn't have a choice,
to leave Gladys, go back to London, that would mean
falling where they had not wanted to go, and it would
be even more difficult without a companion. Birmingham was bourgeois comfort, Mrs William Strether, with
a little weekly outing, the pub as a couple, a dance from
time to time, it seems people enjoyed watching them
dance.

<h2 style="text-align:center">115</h2>

'I had changed my addiction, Max,' said Gladys, 'simply
changed my addiction, instead of being addicted to the
Thames, at night, to being addicted to lying, the fear
of being unmasked makes you ingenious, you know.

'When I returned from Birmingham, to London, I remained a colonel, I found a job as a clerk at an insurance company but it grew increasingly difficult, the company didn't have a lot of money, it couldn't borrow, its debtors didn't pay, I could have been fired at any moment.

'At the office there were a lot of veterans, a few from Mons, I quickly realized that they didn't have any true stories to tell, they hadn't been at the centre of the fighting. At first I was very discreet, I confirmed two or three details, I corrected many which had been confirmed by others, I had real documentation, I had learnt to make index cards when I wanted to be a teacher, that helped.

'In Birmingham, I had already begun to tell the story of Mons, picking up Mark's stories, groping around, I quickly understood why he spoke of a special unit, he said he'd been put at the disposition of headquarters, you call that the irregular forces, don't you? He'd never been a member, but he hardly risked confronting a man from the same regiment as the one he was claiming for himself, the best thing in those cases is to have belonged to a unit that didn't exist, a phantom unit, like the angels, and to never give the impression that you are boasting, I even spoke of inglorious episodes, bouts of trembling, a month of trembling after a bombing, it was easy, I had only to describe what I'd seen in the field hospitals and to attribute that to myself, I spoke of my panic at the idea of going back to the

HÉDI KADDOUR

front, I invented the two fears, the fear of dying and the fear of being found unworthy on the front by the troops, and I made myself go back into battle.'

116

Why was Strether believed for so long? Now that the truth had been revealed, everyone realized that there was constantly something to doubt, that hoarse voice, those slightly long eyelashes, that modesty in the changing room, that knowledge of women, that posture, sometimes, when the hero of Mons wasn't paying enough attention to his pelvis.

Max had an explanation. He had met with Strether often, had been tricked often, and he of course had an explanation.

'Why was I taken in? Because Strether began to talk to me about Fascism and knights, that's when I really became interested, a desire for the report, those recesses of history, that brotherhood, the trips to Germany, that became a real story. When you're told of a nocturnal arrival at a Bavarian castle, the flames, the shadows, the swords, you want to embellish it, the shadows on the walls, the drafts and the reddish glow of the brazier, you step out of the report, you delve into the novel, the great genre, and ultimately it's not a lie, you're not leaving the truth, you know Blake? William Blake, the *Proverbs of Hell*? There's one I really like, *Truth can never be told so as to be understood, and not be believ'd,* that's where Strether led me, to the desire to write something in which I could make the truth be believed, before calling it true. I didn't fall into the lie, I became intoxicated with the truth.'

117

And many people, according to Max, also needed to believe in Strether. He had become the character in the scene everyone needed.

It was difficult to explain but, especially this last year, when he didn't attend a meeting there was always someone who said, 'Someone's missing, it's Strether.' They needed him, not as a presence but because his absence created a void. When he was there, both meek and whole, in clothes that were borderline precious, not the type to pick his nose or touch his crotch in front of others, when he was there people were more careful of themselves, as they would have been in front of a lady, and they thought it was because he was a hero. Add to that that the English Fascists still lacked true personalities, for once they had one, a hero of the battlefield, they wanted to believe in their hero of the battlefield, and Strether was the perfect one. Especially since he wasn't a threatening hero, he didn't seek to force himself onto them, to grab power from the other leaders. Max hesitated, smiled, even finally said that when he was telling the story 'He wasn't a predator, not an ordinary tough guy.'

118

Strether himself, added Max, was very careful not to go where he might be caught out. He never joined the official association of veterans of Mons, the best known, the largest. When he was asked why, he said that it was too neutral, one sensed he was trying to remain a gentleman in his judgement, but sometimes he went so far as to say that the association was weakly neutral, that it didn't support the values for which the men had fallen.

And when the members of the said associa- tion indulged in libellous allusions to Strether, it was immediately understood that it was because those people felt threatened by the aura of a decisive man who had chosen his side. That had played in Strether's favour—if the enemies questioned his virility, it was because they couldn't attack his heroism.

And then, there really weren't that many who had returned from Mons. It was a battle that occurred in August 1914, from which the survivors had had four years to die in turn. Right after the war, there had been a debate on the battle: Was it a forced retreat, or a voluntary retreat? Had the men fallen facing forward or while fleeing? No one wanted to reopen the debate on the issue.

119

And Lord Raglan, a rather enlightened member of the Conservative Party, revealed another reason, on several occasions, in the reading room of his club. Such a thing would probably never have occurred in a truly organized milieu, where one knows how to detect intruders. And when men have a tendency to open their ranks, to make room in the name of camaraderie and spilt blood, it is the wives who quickly undertake the necessary investigating—there are children to protect, after all, dowries, inheritances to evaluate seriously, the *Who's Who* is an obligation. When you have one or two daughters, fifteen, sixteen years old, you instinctively distrust impostors, you know what to do.

Lord Raglan went back to his reading, his interlocutors hesitated to resume the discussion and began to think of something else, and Lord Raglan's distinctive voice again rose up, 'Yes, we have spent centuries knowing what to do, whereas, coming across as a pure and tough group, the Fascist movement is rather an interloper, isn't it? It is perfect for seducing workers and radicals, it's not part of us, at least as long as we continue to know how to behave.'

It had been an opportunity for Strether, to live and act in an inattentive milieu, in the midst of people who talked a lot but were not distrustful. Lord Raglan was clear—among Fascists, many people had things to hide, one his origins, another the origin of his fortune, a third his true rank in the army, or his degrees, or his true profession, or his feats in the battle of the Somme. No one among those people sought to find out the truth about Strether, about anyone in the organization. When they dealt with their adversaries, it was different, the Fascists spent their time revealing information about their adversaries, the truth became a national obligation. But for their friends, no one was permitted such a thing.

Here Lord Raglan paused again, then resumed, 'And no one did it, because the trouble with the truth is that it is true for everyone.'

120

And when one of Lord Raglan's interlocutors evoked the question of Strether's relationship with the police, Lord Raglan said that it had been Strether's luck, 'Yes, he had a relationship with an inspector, even a superintendent or something like that, you're right, but it was his luck, I mean, that's where the suspicions arose, and it's there that he was quickly exonerated, he wasn't a stool pigeon, on the contrary, he had meetings with the police, he used his relationships in the interest of the party, relationships of a veteran. It was enough.

'That little Fascist movement was simple—you asked your neighbour to believe you, you in turn had to believe him, and one rediscovered the feelings of

August 1914 when the war was going to reinvent life in a great flood of belief.'

Lord Raglan again paused, again resumed, 'To reinvent life out of a lie.'

When he concluded his reflections with those rather cynical words, Lord Raglan kept from accompanying them with a grimace, he wasn't a showman, his face remained impassive, the English said that his upper lip remained stiff, to the point that the interlocutor wondered if he had heard correctly.

Lord Raglan was a knight, had been a member of the guard of honour at Queen Victoria's funeral, he incarnated imperial tradition. But he sometimes said things that went against everything he was, statements of a radical troublemaker, an anarchist, he spoke them in the middle of a conversation, and one wondered if it was a bombshell or a joke.

He hadn't always been like that. But imagine that you are presiding over a patriotic banquet in 1916, that you are going to give the closing speech, that it is the penultimate stage before an important nomination to the services of the ministry of war, the crowning of your career, a career entirely devoted to the throne and the country, in two minutes you are going to go up to the podium, it is a moment of glory, your personal secretary is behind you, he is very upset, the secretary, you have always told him 'The essence of urgency is not to wait' but he has a message for you and he is hesitating.

121

The secretary has precise orders, to open telegrams and to convey them immediately if they're urgent, he opened it, it is urgent of course, but is it urgent enough to interrupt Lord Raglan, perhaps even to upset Lord Raglan, will he be able to use it in the speech he is about to give? The minutes went by very quickly, the secretary hesitated, his boss was going to stand up, the secretary acted impulsively, he handed him the telegram, and Lord Raglan climbed to the podium to exalt the values of the country, of battle, of loyalty while reading the telegram that announced the nomination of an arch enemy to the post promised to him, no, that's not it, the announcement that his two sons had died in battle, that very day, and he climbed the last steps while someone introduced him to the audience, *one of the greats of our tradition of courage and honour, etc*. The time to reread the telegram, put it in his pocket and start his speech against pacifism, the summer of 1916 was the season of offers of negotiation, *we can make the necessary sacrifices but we will not give in to the perverse cries for capitulation, sacrifices*, in the last minute he knew he would have no more to make, that's what struck him, not the pain but the discovery that he was capable of speaking in a strong voice the words that made him want to cry, he had not become an enemy of war, no, he simply wanted to cry, and instead of giving in to that desire he gave the speech.

He had not become a pacifist any more than he had remained a dyed-in-the-wool patriot, no, he continued to be a lord but he no longer committed himself to anything or anyone, he never gave any more speeches, and from time to time, when he felt emerging from his lips a slightly bold word, such as that which he had on the war, life and lies, he did not bite it back.

122

Even among the true veterans of Mons in the party there were some who had not really participated in the battle, or they had been in a place where there hadn't been any fighting, or in another place at the front that was never mentioned.

And so when they talked, people didn't lie, they were content to slide over a few kilometres, a few dozen kilometres, perhaps a hundred, and they admired Strether because Strether had been in the thick of things. Call that a farce, a generalized farce in which no one wants to say 'The emperor has no clothes,' not because they're afraid of the emperor but because in reality we are all more or less naked.

And there is probably more, said Dr Winchell, so as not to allow Lord Raglan to take away the prize for the best explanation. They say you had to be truly blind not to see that the chap was a woman, that really everyone saw it, a man with such smooth skin, it was at least ambiguous, indeed, it was the ambiguity that ensured Strether's strength and duration. A true male impostor, an authoritative impostor, that would have provoked cockfights.

That wasn't the case with Strether, when he looked at you, with his soft voice, his very smooth skin, his slender hands, you didn't want to beat him up, he was of another humanity. With him the issue of gender didn't arise, he put you in another world where that question gave way to other more fundamental ones and something began to change in the image you had of yourself. That was Strether's strength.

123

Strether/Walthers was talked about again, not in London, no, in the provinces, when she got back on stage, and went on tour in the Midlands, but it wasn't exactly Shakespeare, not even theatre, it was the stage, of course, with a red dress, scarlet, and long hair. A man put her in a chest and sawed it in half. The woman in the chest reappeared in the dress of a man, the dark grey suit of the colonel, without the DSO, of course. People applauded, she saluted and went into the wings trying not to cry.

There was a complaint from the Guild of Variety Show Artists against the magician who employed her, who was accused of using Strether only because of his *notoriety.* The magician had responded that the complaint was unfair, that Mrs Walthers had been hired only for the requirements of the show, a show of illusions, and a person who had so magically succeeded as a transvestite should be considered as a master in the art of creating illusion, the heart of the subject, it wasn't that inconvenient fame that today most often prevented Mrs Walthers from finding work, no, the heart of the matter was the success of the show that she had offered for years to a vast audience. Not to mention that Mrs Walthers for a long time worked among show people, she'd had a small career in the theatre. The magician specified that he had even decided to pay Strether twice the minimum wage that she should have earned, only for her qualities of interpretation.

124

What was strangest was that his wife, Marian, the one he had married, who had brought on another accusation, because the bankruptcy of the restaurant as such was not that important, he was accused above all of not having appeared in court, no, what earned him a sentence of twenty months behind bars was his pseudo-marriage with that Marian, one month after their arrival in Birmingham. Do you know what that charming wife declared? That she had always thought Strether was a man. That says a lot about the education and knowledge of life among our young girls. She had grown up in the country, after all, she must have seen sheep, no, she didn't know.

People made fun of that girl but Max knew that the story was more complicated. In her situation it was better for Marian to be a fool than a woman loving another woman. Marian's sadness had struck Max and Lena the day they met her the first time, on Strether's arm, on Westminster Bridge, but Marian had not always been like that. When they met Marian had been very animated, yes, it was Strether himself who told me that, and that she had begun to fade during their stay in Birmingham, Strether said Birmingham as if it was a city like any other and not the one where she had become a man.

Max had one more hypothesis, he was going to use it in his story, you can't have a good story without a hypothesis.

125

Max's hypothesis about Marian was that Marian had become a wife, a housewife. Gladys played the husband, and Marian played the wife, and, since she didn't really know what that meant, she did what she most often saw other wives do—be discontent.

In Birmingham she still had a bit of a social life, she had had to leave the till at the restaurant but she would sometimes go to lend a hand, she had friends in the area, Strether and she sometimes went out at night, after they closed the restaurant. But in London all that changed, Strether worked in the evenings, during the day he had his party activities, Marian became a house-wife, a housekeeper. It was security, she couldn't give it up. Marian's sadness was that intrusion of the man in a couple of girlfriends. Strether worked, his wife had the housework, the shopping, the cooking, the associated conversations, the dullness of domestic life. Apart from security, Marian didn't have much else, she couldn't do like other women, she couldn't rule the home in the name of the famous female realm forbidden to men.

At the time, Lena sensed something, when she said about Strether that he might have played a husband, but one did not sense behind him a woman who pulled the strings.

'Even so,' said Lena, 'that Marian, I don't under-stand how one can stifle oneself like that. Why? So the other can go out and be clever in the world? You'll say it's female weakness, female character to sacrifice one-self, to give, to help, to comfort, to support . . .' Lena's voice had grown harder, 'Yes, Gladys must have played on that, shown true suffering, made it known that she needed warmth, security, attention each time she came back home. She had come from the edge of a pit, she needed softness, that's another word for docility, and Marian must have wanted to give all that, you know why you're not contradicting me, Max? Because you're horrible!'

And Max answered that they didn't know anything, that Marian had never spoken to anyone, that Lena was making all that up.

126

A few years later, when the story was forgotten, Max and Lena met in Paris, a dinner at the restaurant in the Gare de Lyon where Max was then going to get a night train for Rome. The elections of 1936 had just brought the Popular Front to power, women were climbing to the ranks of ministers. 'Under ministers,' said Lena, 'and women still don't universally have the right to vote.'

They concluded their tour of the political horizon. Lena had surprised Max with her knowledge of what was going on in Germany, 'but stop talking about it, Max, it's making me really depressed.'

They now turned to feelings and, to make Max mad, Lena reminisced out loud and tenderly about her Rubato. 'In the end, I wasn't nice, he was in the midst of an *éducation sentimentale*, that boy, I hope his novelist treated him better than I, he must be happy, it's likely, you don't hear about him as a pianist any more.'

Lena as a modest woman. And Max made a point of not contradicting her because that was what she expected, contradiction, she wanted to hear him confirm that she had made a mistake, that Thibault was a fool, a passing fancy, you can't always control one's appetites, but Max thought that he would not be repaid if he played that role, so he stayed silent, smiling. Lena was forced to continue, come what may, following the thread of what she had begun, her self-indulgent evocation of a little cretin.

They had finished their main course, the servers had cleared the platter of bones from the roast they had shared, they tidied up the table and put wine in their glasses, Lena had only to change the subject, to abandon Rubato for Strether, and Max perked up, he said, 'Admit it, she ended up pleasing you, that guy?'

'No,' said Lena, 'but I found him interesting. He wasn't that attractive, but for once there was a man who could not be easily explained.'

127

Lena took a large piece of brie and let the waiter walk away with the platter. She pointed out with the tip of her knife the bits of lettuce Max had left on his plate, and she said, 'You still want to be a svelte young man?'

She went back to Strether. What was difficult to explain about that man? 'His scorn for what he called *gold-diggers*, Max. We can understand it today but in London I was intrigued. Ordinary men don't have that scorn for gold-diggers, or maybe a father with an only son to protect. Strether was different, he was really mean, whereas you, I mean ordinary men, when you talk about that sort of girl one senses that they amuse you, you hesitate to say anything really mean, you attribute them with know-how, now don't act sceptical, you want details? I first thought Strether must have been in love with a gold-digger who left him when she saw he didn't have a penny. But it wasn't that, it wasn't resentment. I've seen the same thing among singers in mid-career, when they speak of singers who never get beyond operetta and who work in music halls in Belgium, as duos, with a guy who colours his hair. And it is only now that I understand Strether's scorn, anger, it's that she must have come very close to the brink, and when she said gold-diggers she was obviously thinking of *hookers*, *whores*. Her masculine scorn was that of a woman, an escapee, she was speaking of gold-diggers the way English males speak of homosexuals when they've finally escaped the school dormitories. For her, it was the scorn of the sheep that was able to stay on the bridge when the others jumped off and were drowned without realizing it.'

128

'If I may,' said Max, stabbing the piece of brie that Lena had just cut off, 'the story is even more complicated. Gladys became a veteran to survive, and behind the mask she scorned men. That's what she was telling us, that she dressed as a man so as not to become the final chapter in a bad novel, but that's for the lawyer, it's a plea. In reality, one cannot live every day as a character one hates.'

'What became of her?' asked Lena.

'After the stint in the music hall, she continued as a man, she sold cars at Ford, a good salesman, fired for economic reasons, then as a woman, she had a relationship with a shopkeeper, she made off with some hundred pounds, again as a man, on a stud farm, fired as a true man, for alcoholism, then as a woman, on a chicken farm, that didn't work. I heard from her not long ago, again as a woman, after a trial where she succeeded in getting off with two years of probation. She is head chef in Kent. She seems to be doing better. Marian has joined her. They are like many, they can't stand the pleasure of being alone.'

Lena didn't answer. Max sat back, sinking into his seat, looking round the dining room, 'You know what really happened to her? She began to like the role that was saving her, that is the secret of Strether, and the sadness of Marian.'

'Max, don't be a fool, she didn't like being a man!'

'No, but she didn't leave much space for Marian. In the couple, she was the one who performed. That said, there is something else . . .'

Max again looked round the room, too bad, there was another idea that he wanted to keep to himself for a while, because he didn't understand it very well, it came from a letter from Gladys, an idea that contradicted the statement he had just made, but he offered it to Lena, for the good of the discussion, 'Not long ago, she wrote to me that she loved what she had done but that she had never thought as a man, she watched them watching her, she took hold of their ideas, of their mannerisms, to better advance herself, to gather into her head the ideas that they put out there, to take what she never mentioned when she was with women—the world, yes, the world, the intoxication of finally being able to speak about the world, to act in the world, that's what she wrote, and you're going to like the rest, she said that, behind Strether she had been much more of a woman than if she had stayed a woman.'